U0935673

我的我的天

应霁漫画前传

outthere

欧阳应霁 著

目次　　Contents

前言	Forword	4
去死	To Die	16
早晨	Good Morning	18
都是他的错	It's All His Fault	20
大气候	The Climate	22
示威	Demonstration	24
隔壁的男人	The Man Next Door	26
过程	Process	28
风景	View	30
病	Ill	32
三个为什么?	Why?Why?Why?	34
惊梦	Nightmares	36
地球之友	Friend of the Earth	38
打击	Attack	40
休息	Rest	42
白梦	Dream Blanks	44
烦	Tediousness	46
小睡	Nap	48
赌	Bet	50
他和癞蛤蟆	He and the Toad	52
了解	Understand	54
永无忧	No Risk	56
石头记	The Story of The Stone	58
雨	Rain	60
我	Self	62
情事	Love Affairs	64
日记	Diary	66
这一个夜	Tonight	68
听说	I was Told……	80
咒	Curse	82
最新不了情	The Latest Romance	84
原则	Principle	86
思想起	Remember	88
沙滩的一天	A Day On the Beach	90
遗嘱	The Will	92
得失记	Lost and Found	94
行李	Luggage	96
困	Trapped	98
鲜花和鲜血	Flowers and Blood	100

烟火夜	The Night of the Fireworks	102
信	Letter	104
水果先生	Mr.Fruits	106
另一种情书	Love Letter of Another Kind	108
猫或沙发	The Cat And The Sofa	110
恐龙与蚂蚁	The Dinosaur And The Ants	112
铁甲老人	Mr.Old Robot	114
等	Wait	116
天外来	From Outer Space	118
问题	Problem	120
如果在冬夜一件行李	If On A Winter's Night a Suitcase	122
家事	Housework	124
手	Hands	126
礼	Gift	128
杂耍	Vaudeville	130
魔术	Magic	132
沉思者	Thinker	144
飞人	Flying Man	146
记挂	Cares	148
哭笑之间	Between Laughing and Crying	150
过日子	Pastime	152
路	Road	154
别人	Someone Else	156
大扫除	Clean up	158
后事	Afterwards	160
罪	Sin	162
做人难	It's a Difficult Life	164
活着	To Live	166
晚间新闻	Evening News	168
遗痕	Leaving Marks	170
借口	Cause	172
新年愿望	New Year's Resolution	174
生趣	The Fun of Life	176
愿	Three Wishes	178
多谢	Thanks	180
历史性访问	A Historic Interview	182
结果	Fruitless	184
回家	Home Sweet Home	186
看海的日子	Room with a Sea View	188
后记	Afterword	200

前言

我的天

在地上走路，瞻前顾后，跌跌撞撞或快或慢。

间歇停下来站一站，坐一坐，
四周自然的人工的风景流过，看过——

然后抬头看天。

天上有黑白彩色，有虚实形态，有远近距离。
转眼高矮肥瘦，瞬间风雷雨电，
一场家常便饭，一局流血革命，一回咳嗽感冒……
在界线和规矩的有与无当中，浮躁的天使和神圣的妖孽交手交心，
天上有机会。

从地下往上看天，从天上往下看地，满足同时遗憾，同样有趣。
我看漫画，漫画看我；我画，画我。

这本集子收录的作品，源起自许多年前在台北的半载勾留。
四格八格接接续续在台北的一份晚报上发表，
后来转在香港一份日报里出现，
又再延伸发表在台北另一份日报，至今未断。

他城我城的种种经验和记忆，轻的浮的沉的重的，
都在这格与格之间交叠，衍生，反照，变形……
之后两城匆匆往来，聚会间旧友给我介绍新知，
都以“他就是那个画那些漫画的”称呼，又感动又惭愧。

此时此间，漫画不是、不敢是我的全部、我的天。
因为怕一旦“专业”带来的种种限制，
怕这些黑白文字图像过分自大充斥满天之际，
没有空间给漫画自己本身生长，
没有机会给漫画与其他媒体发生关系。
私家的昨天今天明天，不求亦难求一个全貌：
昨天历史与明天未来同样不可信不可测，
今天现在似乎变得最真实，过渡是一种每天的游戏，
有意无意自生自灭，看来是目前这批漫画的状态。

我相信，漫画作为一种表达情感的工具（作为一种感情？），
兼收并蓄然后孑然一身，什么也是什么也不是：
最有韧性最有弹性，最鲜活最高贵，最轻佻，最贱。

各人头上一片天，各自精彩。
当天黑了累了，糊里糊涂的，我们在地下相拥，或哭或笑。

《我的天》初版序　九五年七月

第一次投稿，第一回领稿费，
第一个每日连载专栏，第一本漫画单行本，
一步一个脚印，走上漫画不归路。

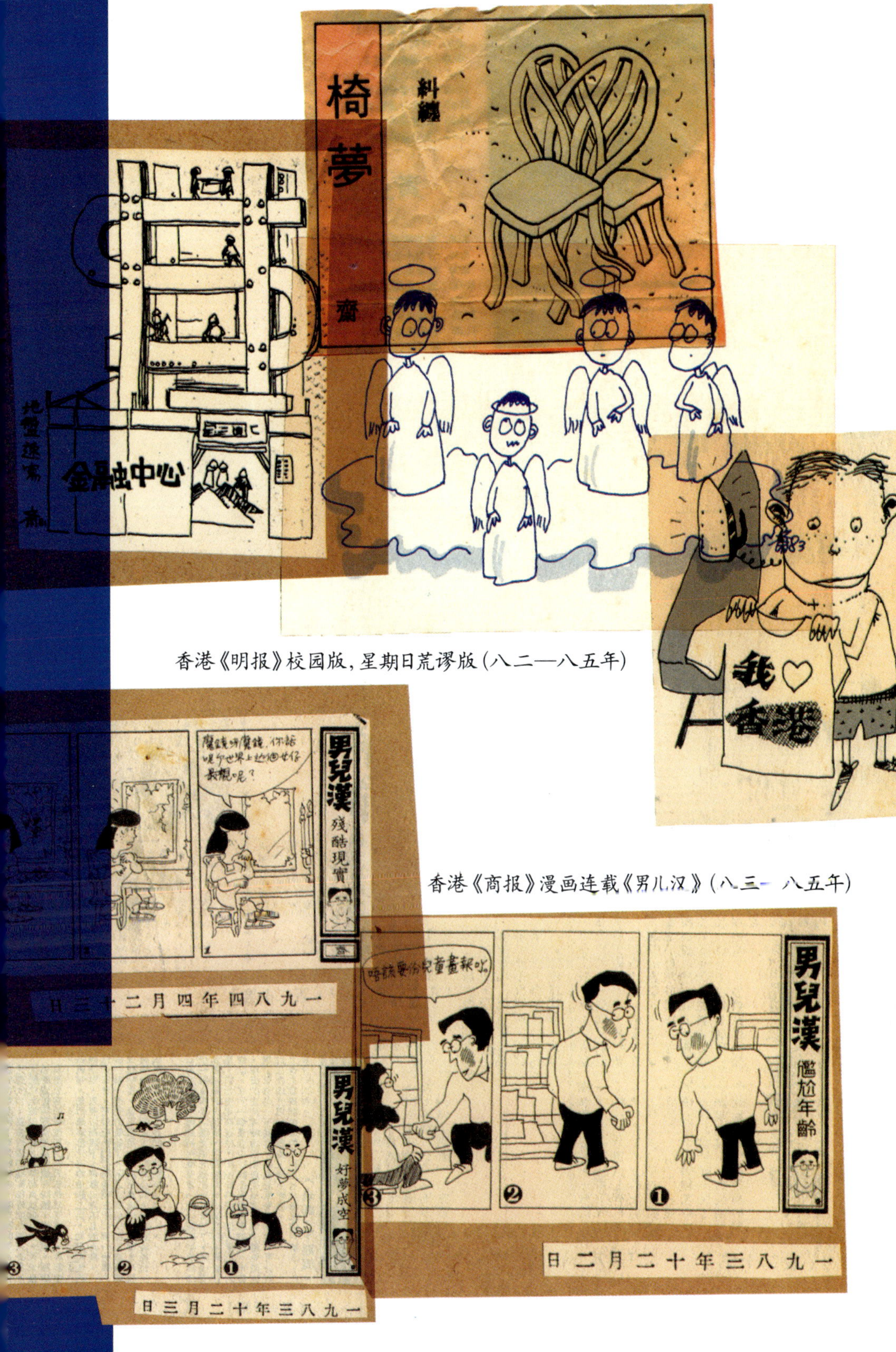

香港《明报》校园版，星期日荒谬版（八二—八五年）

香港《商报》漫画连载《男儿汉》（八三—八五年）

香港《博益月刊》漫画连载《城市男人》(八七—八八年)

香港《学生时代》漫画连载
《呢班人》(八五—八六年)

香港《新一代双周刊》漫画连载《故事新编》(八六—八七年)

漫画个展《A Boy's Own Story》(八五年/香港)

香港《号外》杂志漫画连载(九〇年)

P.1

煙三文　　　　　　　　　　　　　　　　　　　　　　應霽

十分，是下班的時候了

cullus，他跟那个售貨的女子說要煙三文，二百

皆皆的，他只想着待会躺在armchair上一个人懶

，门一推，灯竟是亮着的

沙上好好的坐着一个他从未認識的男子

正要个伴，也就把煙三文大方的遞过去

这样滔滔的談起来，談的是smoked salmon与smoked

的分别

那他们也就睡着了

班的時候了，始終是Luculus的煙三文又便宜又

推开门，眼前竟又是昨天那个男子和另一个从未

認識的女子。

一他有点纳闷，但看见这对男女談得这么投契，他也高兴

的跟他们一起吃着煙三文

一第三天下班，回家推门进去，热闹得很

一熟悉的屋里除了昨天的一对，满眼盡是陌生的男男女女

P.2

只好在仙人掌旁边吃着

的煙三文还是整整齐齐的

个gms

，睡房和厕所都塞満陌生人

黏黏的一片一片放进

香港《号外》杂志漫画连载《连环途》（八七—八九年）

《连环途》单行本（八九年）

面对欧阳应霁的漫画，就像面对端上桌的甜酒热冰淇淋一样，
虽然是我们所熟悉的冰淇淋，但又似乎拥有着一种不可解的面貌
——热冰淇淋，自相矛盾。

还不曾被热冰淇淋感动过的我，已经有好几次被欧阳应霁的
漫画感动了。欧阳应霁出过一本比支票还长的《连环途》，
里面我最喜欢的像《神奇果冻》、《医生早安》都是脆弱又寂寞的、
微微呼吸着的黑白小世界。

我也喜欢欧阳应霁的《我的天》。
《我的天》里面的人，变得更甜美、更善体人意。

真是美丽的、不知道在想什么、
可是没事我就想看两眼的、我的天。

——蔡康永　九六年

去死

To Die

一大清早起来想去死，
然後想想死之前最後應該做什麼？
想来想去竟然沒有什麼東西值得做，
看看手錶又是上班的時候了。

He gets up in the morning and wants to die.
Then he thinks of what he should do before he dies.
After a lot of thinking, he couldn't figure out anything worth doing
He takes a look at his watch, and realises it's time to go to work again.

去死

一大清早起来想去死，
然后想想死之前最后应该做什么？
想来想去竟然没有什么东西值得做，
看看手表又是上班的时候了。

早晨
Good morning

清早起来跟鳥兒說聲早，
給陽台外的花花草草澆滿水，
把房間收拾得清潔整齊出門上班去，
有一塊從天而降的磚頭和他在街角相遇。

Get up in the morning and greets the birds,
Water the plants in the balcony.
Makes up the room nicely and goes to work,
A brick falling from the sky greets him
at the turn of the corner.

早晨

清早起来跟鸟儿说声早，
给阳台外的花花草草浇满水，
把房间收拾得清洁整齐出门上班去，
有一块从天而降的砖头和他在街角相遇。

都是他的錯

It's All His Fault

他從來沒做對過一件事，
例如把整瓶不潔的礦泉水喝光；
一邊接收幅射一邊吃進太多的人造色素；
以及吸入過量的一氧化碳……

He has never done anything right,
Like drinking up a whole bottle of
contaminated mineral water;
Exposing himself to radiation while
Swallowing abundances of
artificial colourings;
And inhaling too much carbon monoxide.

都是他的错

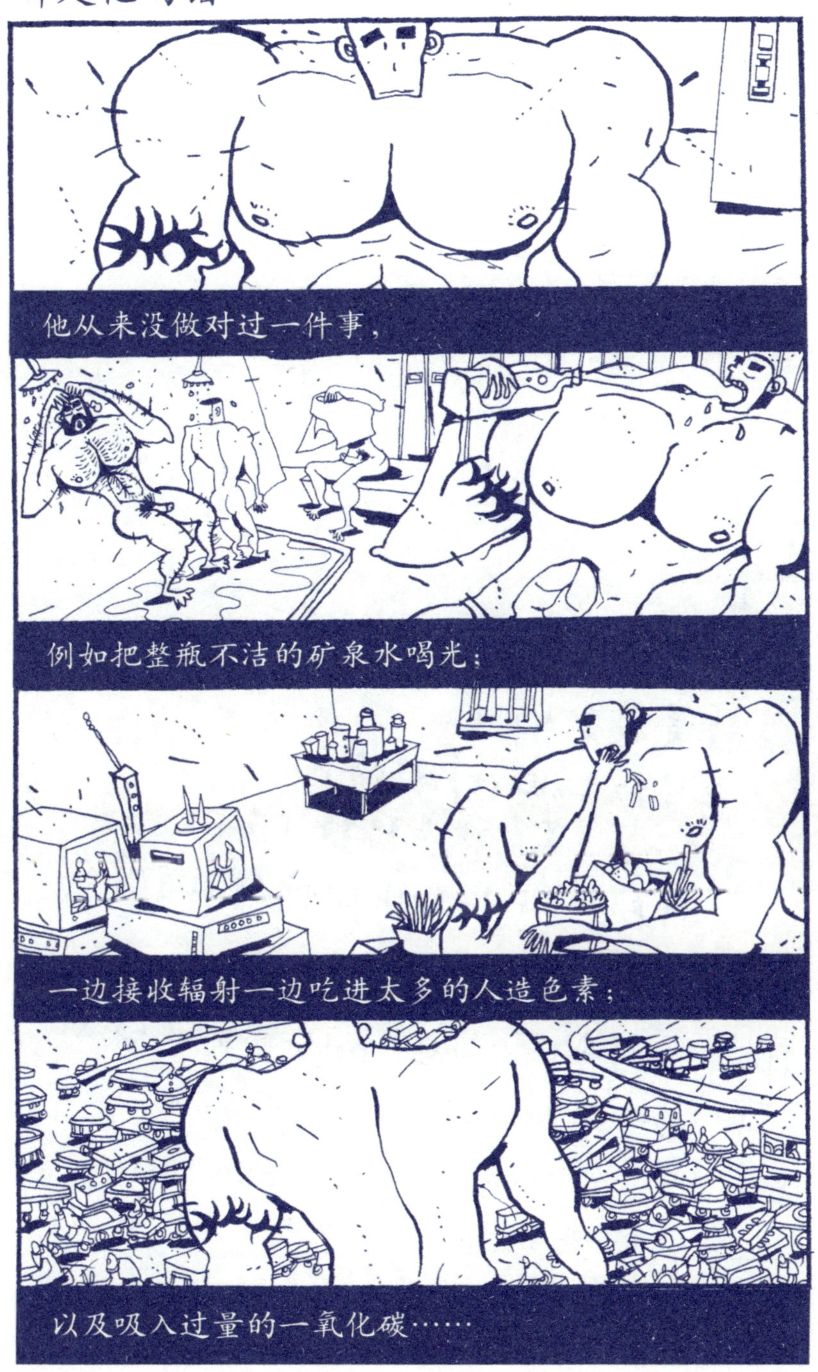

他从来没做对过一件事，
例如把整瓶不洁的矿泉水喝光；
一边接收辐射一边吃进太多的人造色素；
以及吸入过量的一氧化碳……

大氣候
The climate

手臂實在是太累了，
希望找一個休息的時間。
可是成千上萬人還是堅持下去，
作為一份子他只好繼續舉起手臂。

He is very tired indeed holding up his hand.
He hopes to have a rest for a while.
But thousands of people are holding on.
Being one of the people, he has to go on.

大气候

示威
Demonseration

他決定上街示威.
抗議生活太奔波太疲累太無奈.
可是滿街都是示威的人
太熱鬧太擁擠太嘈吵.
他只好乖乖的走回家。

He decides to go to the streets
and demonstrate.
Protesting against the hardship.
the weariness and the futility of life.
But he finds there are too many demonsterators
in the streets. It is too noisy and too crowded
So he goes home quietly

示威

隔壁的男人

The Man Next Door

他一直的跟着我.
凭直觉也知道他有某种意图,
看来要发生的终于要发生,
他原来住在我隔壁。

He follows me all the way.
I know what he wants by a hunch.
The inevitable has to happen somehow.
Well, he turns out to be my neighbour!

隔壁的男人

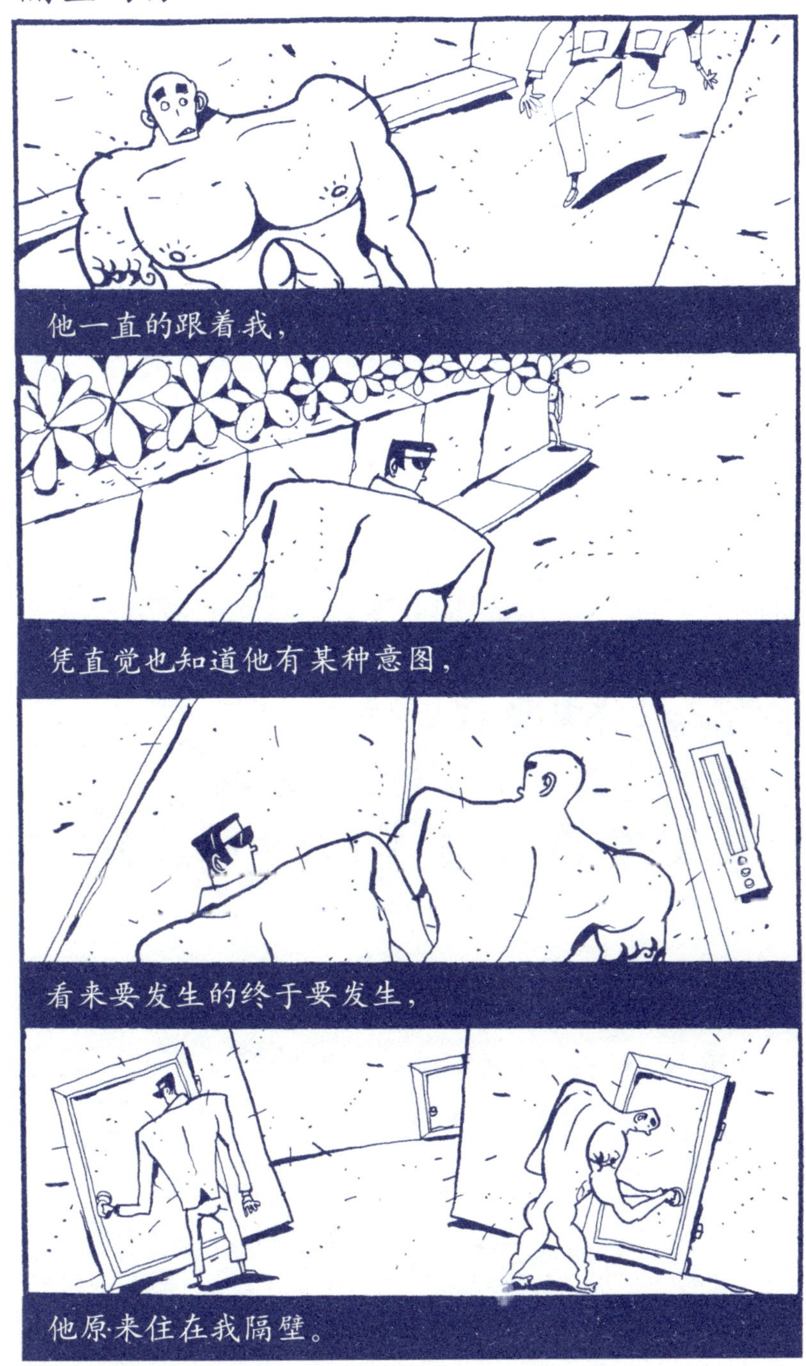

過程
Process

他來自低下層
他因工作需要往上爬．
他在學飛的時候突然想死．
跌得焦頭爛額的時候突然肚餓．

He came from down below.
He has to climb in his work.
He wants to die suddenly as he learns to fly
He hurts himself bad when he falls and he feels hungry all of a sudden.

过程

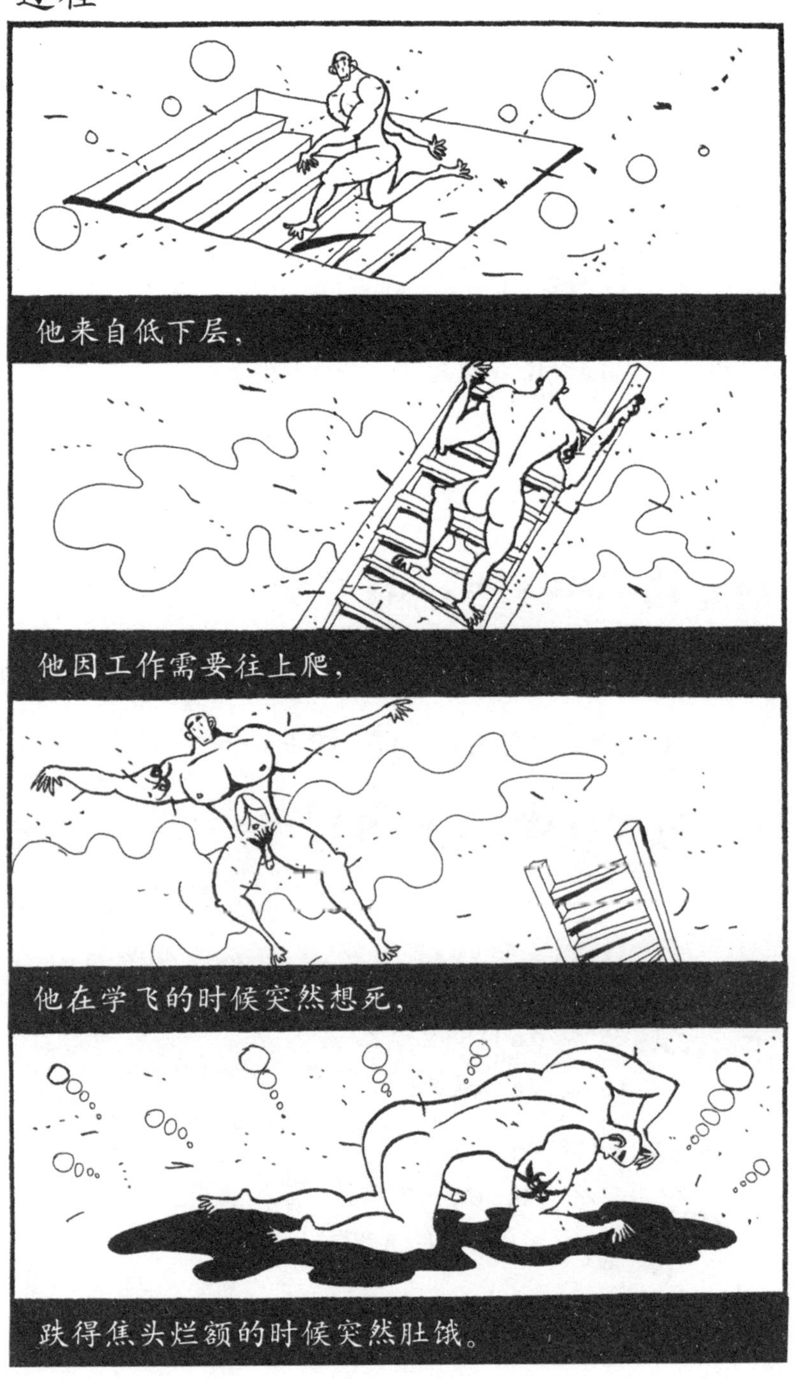

風景

View

他在樓頂站了好一段時候

鬧紛紛的親友和警察都好言相勸。

時機成熟大家都一擁而上——

原來這邊風景獨好。

He has stood on the roof for quite a while.

Friends and policemen come

to give advice and comforts.

They all rush up to him at the right moment.

Only to find out the view

is exceptonally good there.

风景

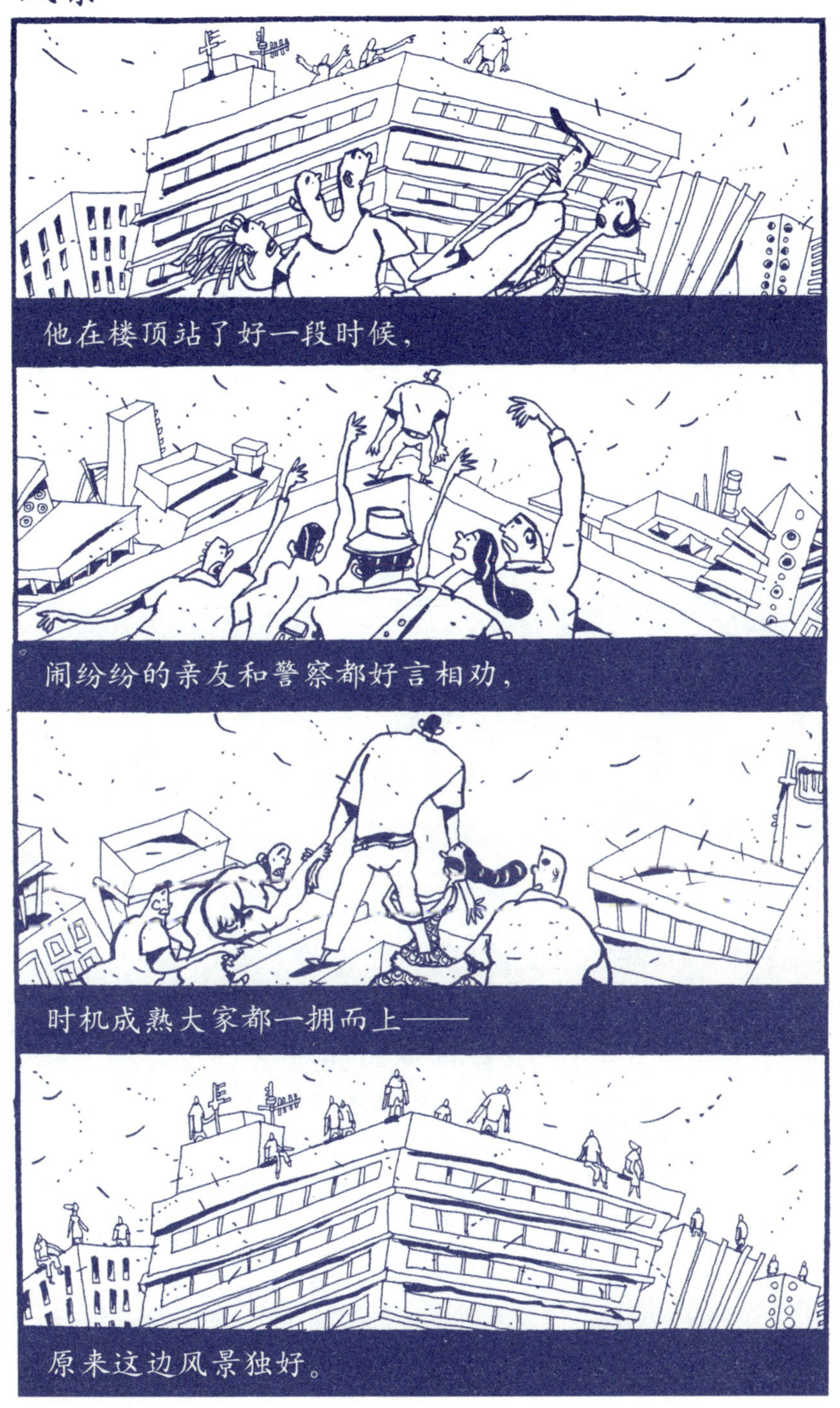

病

ILL

他渴望狠狠的大病一場，
病得所有有心的朋友早晚來探望．
病得把所有的過去都一一忘掉．
病得有一個永遠幸福快樂的未來。

He hopes to get really very ill.
So ill that his friends would come to visit him day and night
So ill that he could forget all about the past,
So ill that he could live happily ever after.

病

他渴望狠狠的大病一场，
病得所有有心的朋友早晚来探望，
病得把所有的过去都一一忘掉，
病得有一个永远幸福快乐的未来。

三個為甚麼？

why? why? why?

每次學校運動會他就主動告病假
因為他不明白為甚麼一定要在起跑線後起跑，
也不明白為甚麼要等裁判鳴槍後才可以起跑，
更不明白為甚麼最先跑到終點就叫做贏。

He'd report sick every time it is sports day.
Because he doesn't understand why the runner has to get set behind the starting line.
And why the runner could only start after the umpire's shot.
And most of all why the one who reaches the finish line first is the winner.

三个为什么？

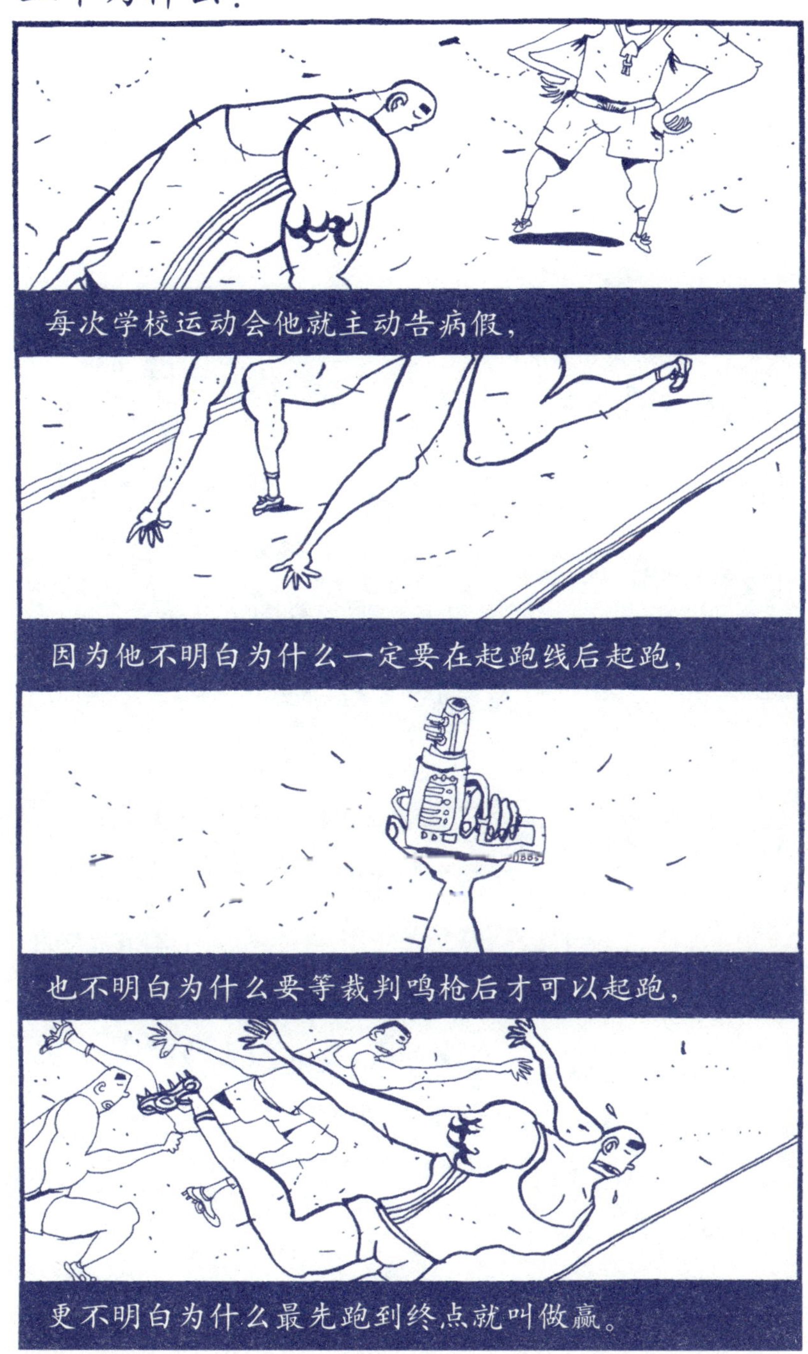
每次学校运动会他就主动告病假，
因为他不明白为什么一定要在起跑线后起跑，
也不明白为什么要等裁判鸣枪后才可以起跑，
更不明白为什么最先跑到终点就叫做赢。

驚夢

Nightmares

星期一午夜他夢到自己被一個從天而降的
衣櫃壓住。

星期二午夜他夢到自己
在地震中從五十樓飛下大街。

星期三午夜他夢到自己坐的客機在高空出了
意外。

星期四午夜他夢到自己跟心愛的女友
終於幸福地踏進教堂。

On Monday night, he dreamt that he has
crushed by a closet falling from above.

On Tuesday night, he dreamt that he
fell from
the 50th floor to the ground
during an earthquake.

On Wednesday night, he dreamt that
he had a plane crash.

On thursday night, he dreamt that he and
his beloved girlfriend were happily married
in a church.

惊梦

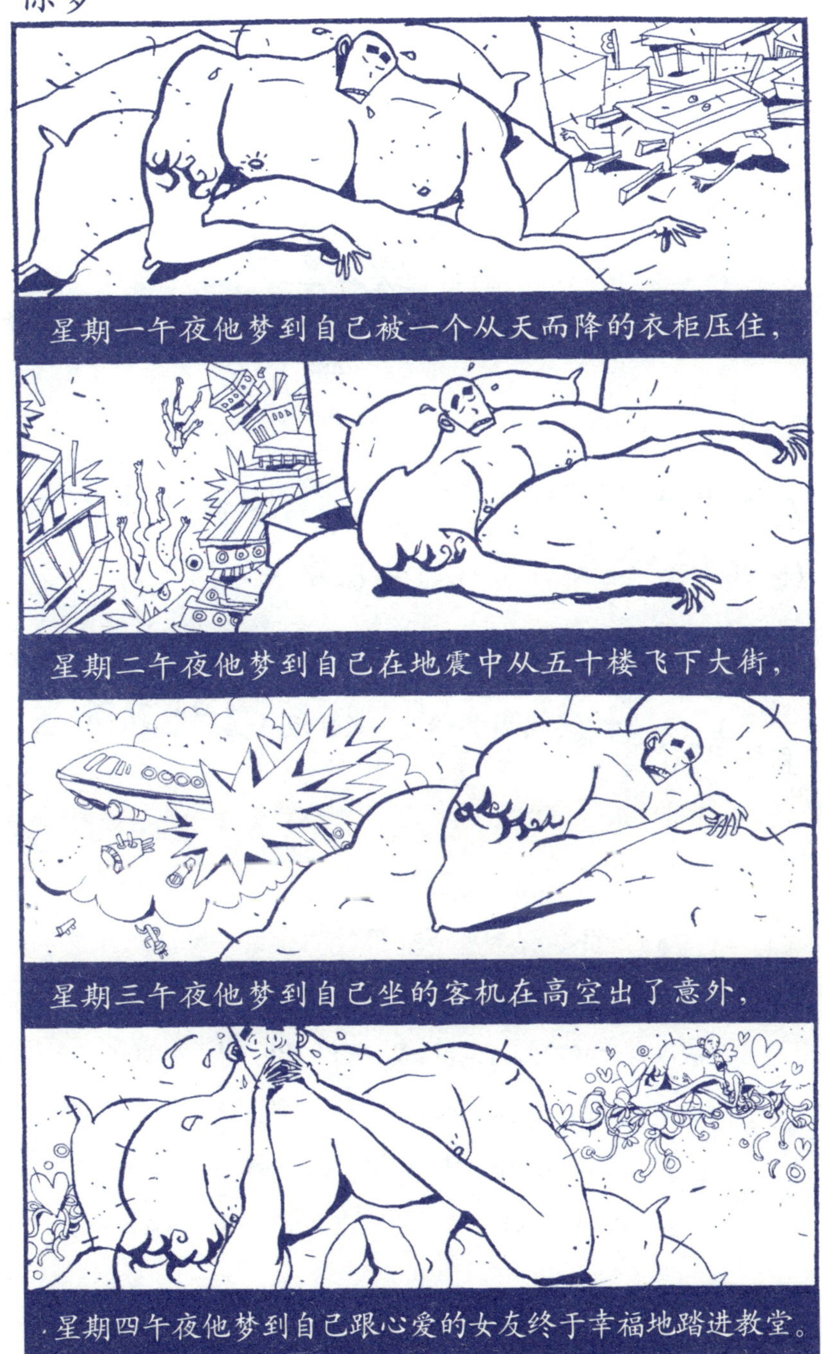

星期一午夜他梦到自己被一个从天而降的衣柜压住，
星期二午夜他梦到自己在地震中从五十楼飞下大街，
星期三午夜他梦到自己坐的客机在高空出了意外，
星期四午夜他梦到自己跟心爱的女友终于幸福地踏进教堂。

地球之友

Friend of the Earth

他是如此的愛地球，
他把地球放在貼在房門和客廳和廁所
和穿在身上，
他為地球的安危盡心盡力歇斯底里。
直至有一天他移情別戀，發現了某顆新星。

He loves the world so much.
So much that he puts it in his sitting room,
dining room, toilet and on his back.
He fights hysterically in saving the world.
Until one day he falls in love
with another newly found star.

地球之友

他是如此的爱地球，
他把地球放在贴在房门和客厅和厕所和穿在身上，
地球
VEOUREARTH
SON OF THE EARTH
他为地球的安危尽心尽力歇斯底里，
直至有一天他移情别恋，发现了某颗新星。

打擊
Attack

沒有信，
門鈴也沒有响，
終於有電話
受不起人家打錯電話的打擊，不接算了。

There is not a letter,
The door bell doesn't ring
and eventually there is a telephone call.
But he can't accept the fate of someone
dialing a wrong number.

打击

休息

Rest

作為旅行團的領隊
他卻是如此的喜歡睡覺。
'其實天下風光都一樣,'他對團員們說。
'其實旅行的目的是休息。'他提醒大家。

He is a tour guide.
But he loves to sleep very much.
So he tells his group members, Actually the scenery is the same everywhere.
And he reminds, Actually, the purpose of a trip is to get some rest.

休息

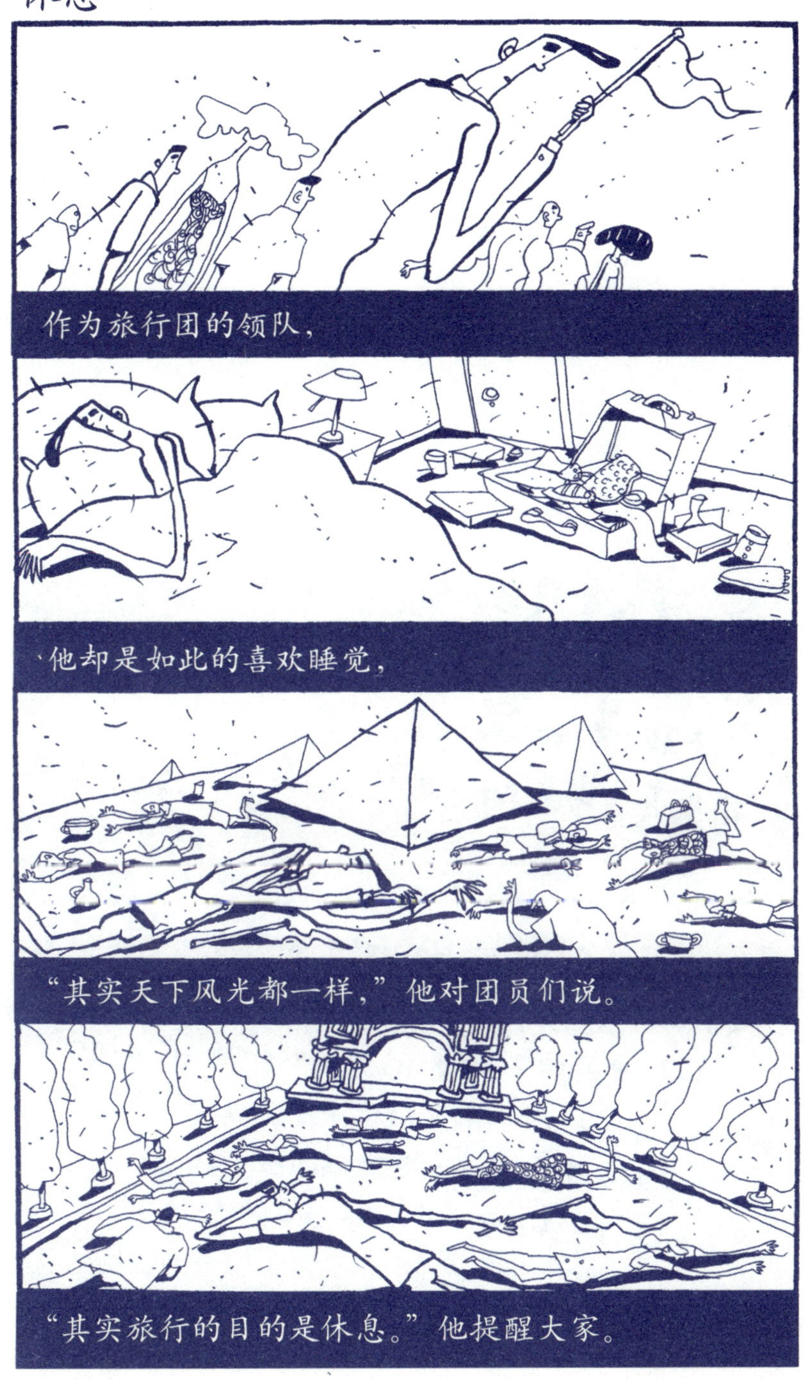

白夢
Dream Blanks

白天實在是發生了太多的事，
到了晚上真的不知該讓甚麼入夢？
半夜驀地驚醒過來
因為夢與夢之間，竟然出現了半小時的空白。

Too many things happen during the day.
So many that it is difficult to choose
what to let into his dreams at night,
Wake up in the middle of the night,
Because he finds there is a
half an hour blank between his dream.

白梦

白天实在是发生了太多的事，
到了晚上真的不知该让什么入梦？
半夜蓦地惊醒过来，
因为梦与梦之间，竟然出现了半小时的空白。

煩
Tediousness

一拿起書來讀他就睡着，
一睡着他就發夢，
一發夢就夢到自己在讀書，
醒來他覺得自己很麻煩。

Once he picks up a book to read, he falls asleep
Once he falls into sleep, he starts to dream.
Once he starts to dream, he dreams of reading a book.
He wakes up and sinks into tediousness

烦

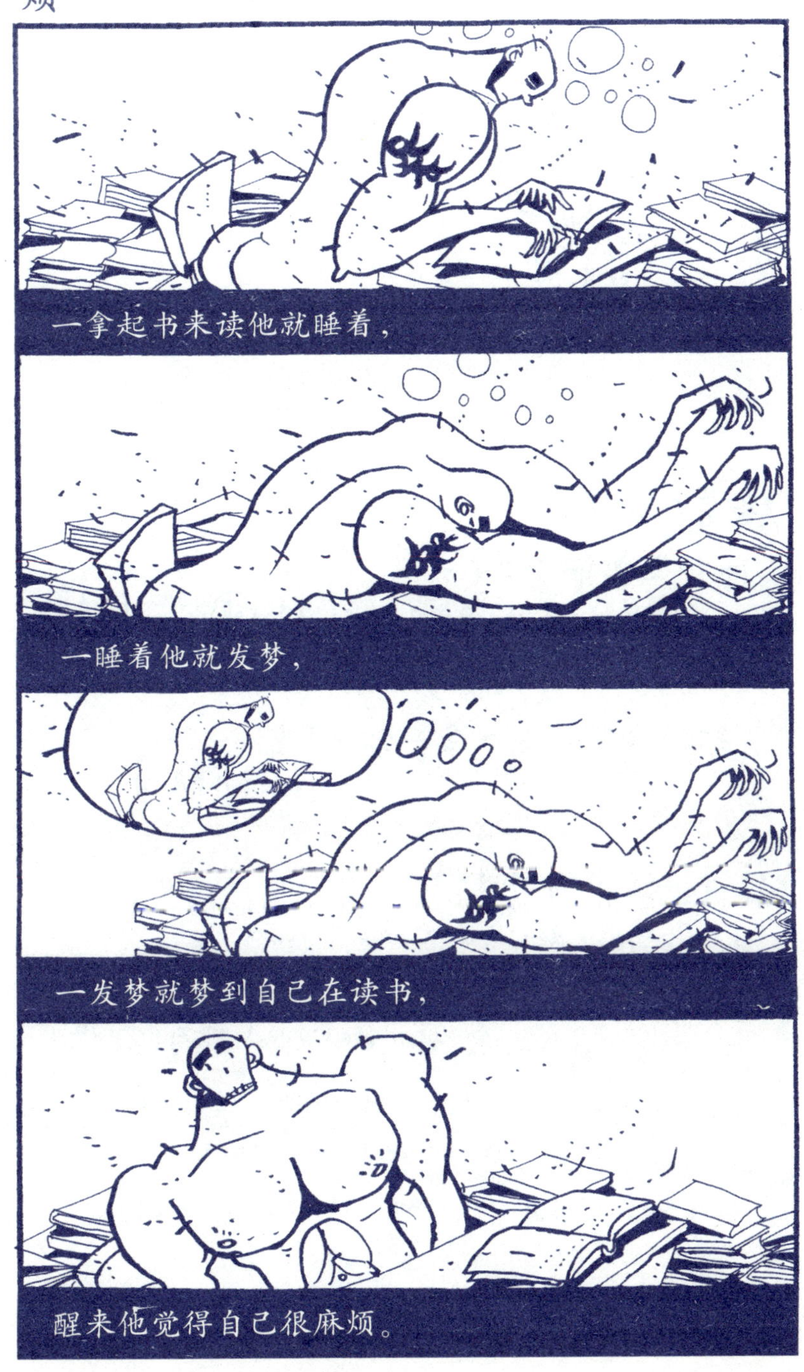

小睡
Nap

他實在太累，
他決定要躺下睡一睡。
雖然作為一間有四千員工的跨國公司的總裁
這樣做有點那個——
但是短短十五分鐘的小睡
大抵不礙事。

He is so very tired
So he decides to take a nap.
It may seem a little bit too much for a
president of an international organisation
with 4000 staff members to do so.
But it would do nobody any harm
to take a nap of 15 minutes

小睡

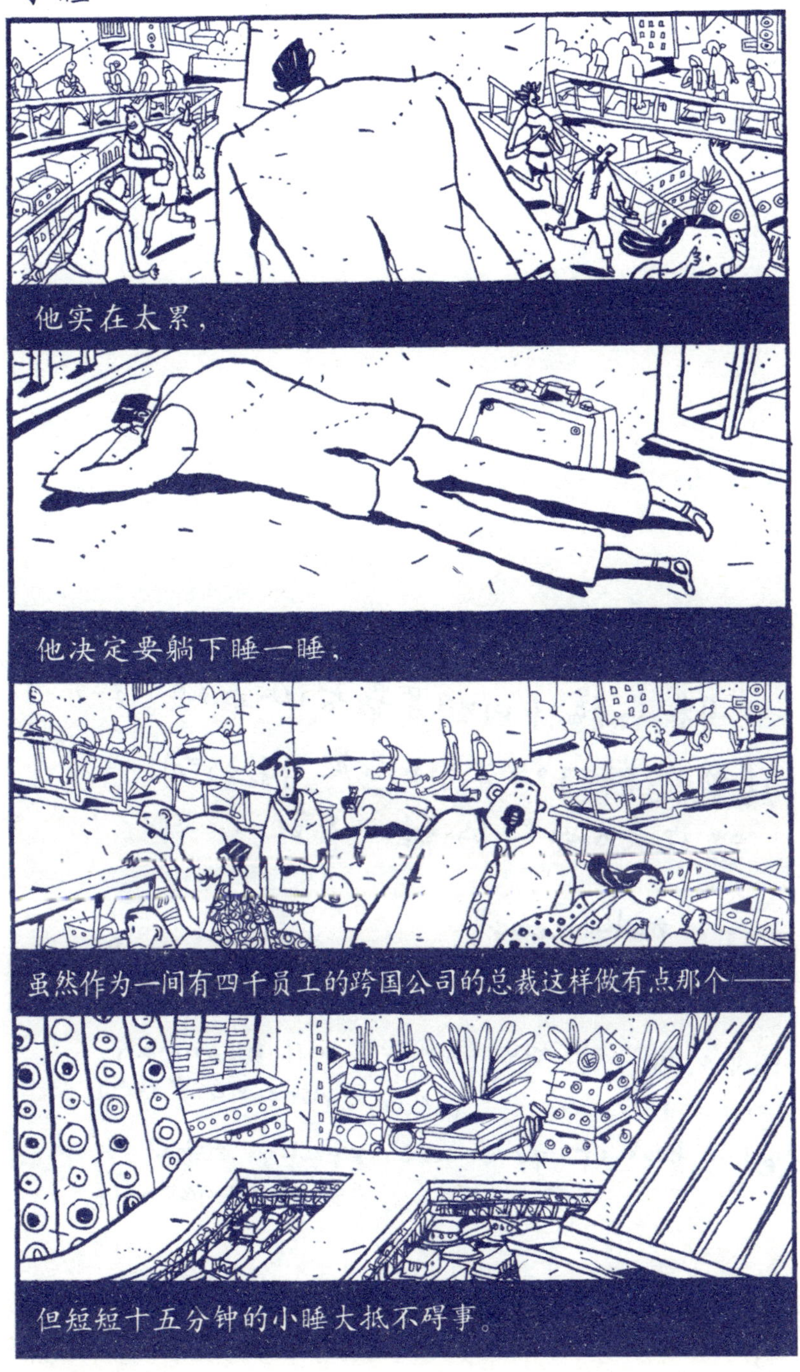

他实在太累，
他决定要躺下睡一睡，
虽然作为一间有四千员工的跨国公司的总裁这样做有点那个——
但短短十五分钟的小睡大抵不碍事。

賭

Bet

就狠狠的來賭一鋪

賭太陽下山明早最否依舊爬上來，

賭花兒謝了明年是否還是一樣的開，

賭你是否如此的難以忘記。

Let's make a bet.

Let's bet on whether the sun will rise tomorrow

Let's bet if the flowers will bloom as usual the next day.

Let's bet if you are really that unforgettable.

赌

他和癞蛤蟆
He and the Toad.

他突然愛上一個癞蛤蟆，
愛到希望吻牠一下的地步。
一吻之後癞蛤蟆變成公主其實很麻煩，
他寧願承受蛤蟆變作王子的一切後果。

He falls suddenly in love with a toad.
So much that he would like to kiss it.
He would be in deep trouble if the toads
turns into a princess.
He'd rather take the consequence
of it turning into a prince.

他和癞蛤蟆

他突然爱上一个癞蛤蟆，
爱到希望吻它一下的地步，
一吻之后癞蛤蟆变成公主其实很麻烦，
他宁愿承受蛤蟆变作王子的一切后果。

了解

Understand

他(她)們夫婦兩人沒對話已經四年，
當互望一眼已經了解對方，說話是不必要的。
他(她)們最近更開始停止用眼神接觸，
轉而滿足的靜聽對方的心跳。

This couple have not talked to each other
for four years already.
There's no need to talk when they
understand each other just by one look
They have stopped communicating with
their eyes recently.
They'd rather listen silently to each other's
heartbeat instead.

了解

他（她）们夫妇两人没对话已经四年，
当互望一眼已经了解对方，说话是不必要的。
他（她）们最近更开始停止用眼神接触，
转而满足的静听对方的心跳。

永無憂
No Risk

他決定向她承認他是蘇聯間諜，
她也打算不再向他隱瞞她火星人的身份。
他/她們一如往常熱烈的做起愛來，
且發覺一直用安全套其實是多餘的。

He decided to confess to her his identity as a KGB.
She also decided not to hide her secret of being a Martian.
They made love as passionately as always.
They also realised that their using the condoms had been superfluous.

永无忧

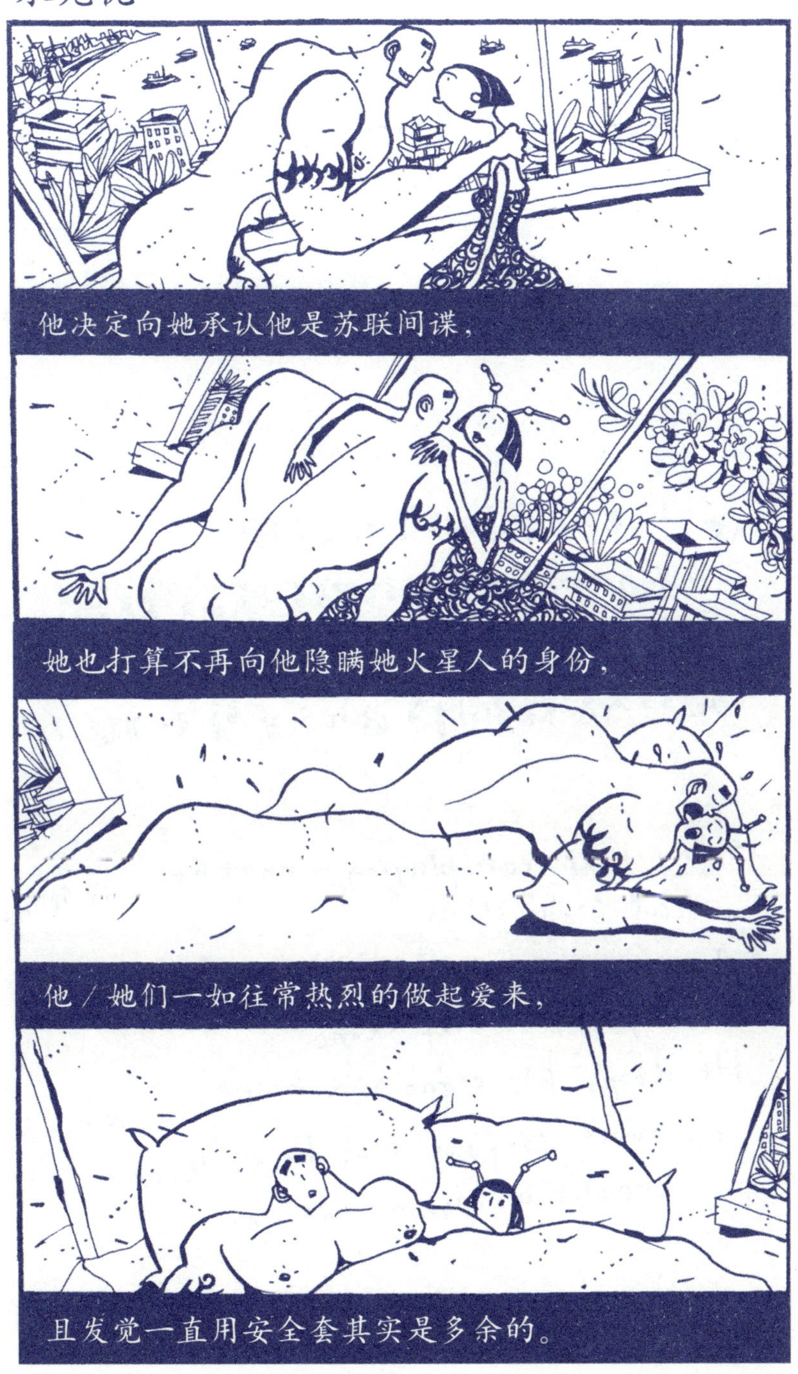
他决定向她承认他是苏联间谍，
她也打算不再向他隐瞒她火星人的身份，
他／她们一如往常热烈的做起爱来，
且发觉一直用安全套其实是多余的。

石頭記
The story of The Stone

他和他玩擲石頭的遊戲．
一不小心他被他的石頭擊中了額頭，
他急忙放下手中石頭跑過去扶他．
走得太急跌倒摔斷了手臂和腿．

They have been playing with throwing stone at each other.

Accidentally he gets hit on the head by a piece of Stone

He drops his stone and rushes to him.

He runs so fast that he falls and breaks his arms and legs

石头记

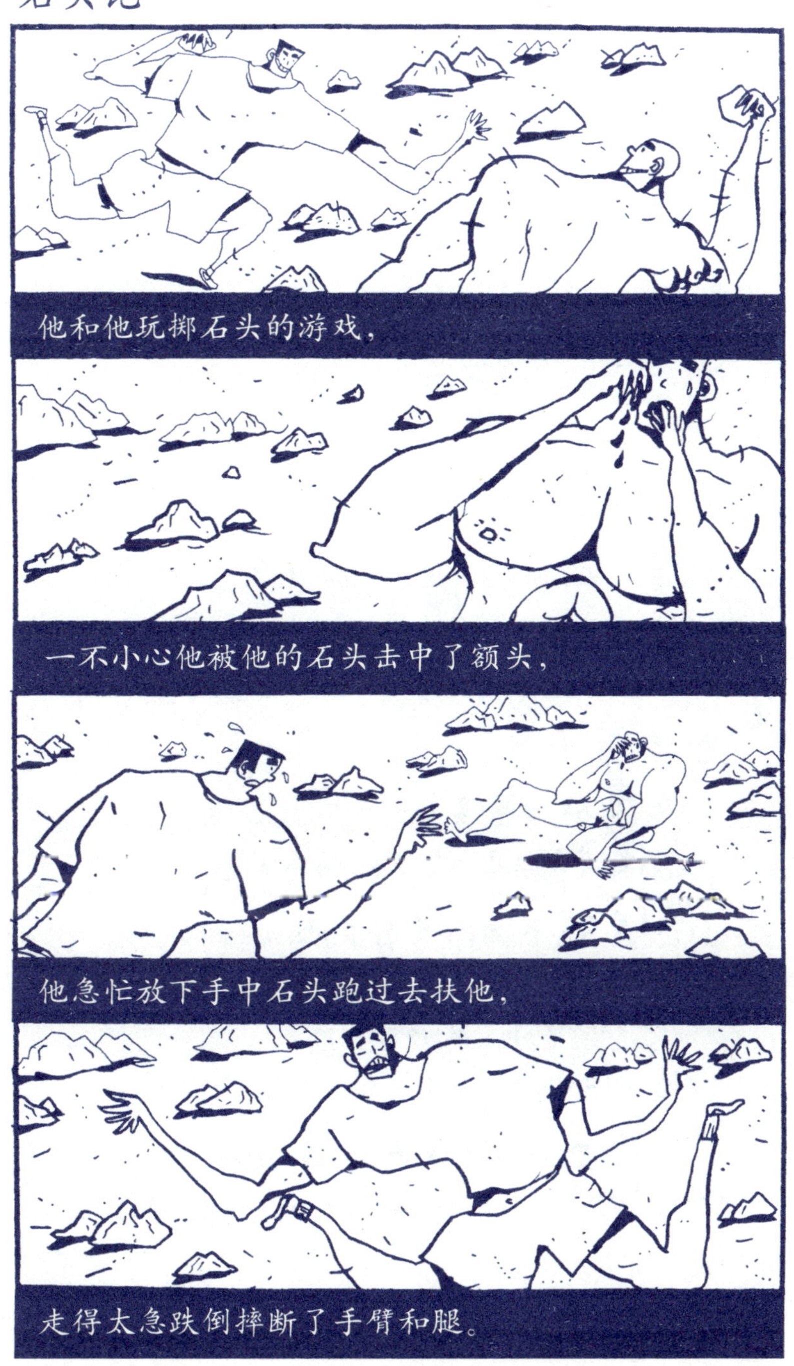
他和他玩掷石头的游戏，
一不小心他被他的石头击中了额头，
他急忙放下手中石头跑过去扶他，
走得太急跌倒摔断了手臂和腿。

雨

Rain

他化作泥，

他變成種子，

他把自己投進他裡面，

然後很久都沒有下雨。

He turns into dust

He changes into seeds.

He throws himself into him.

and there is no rain for a long period of time.

雨

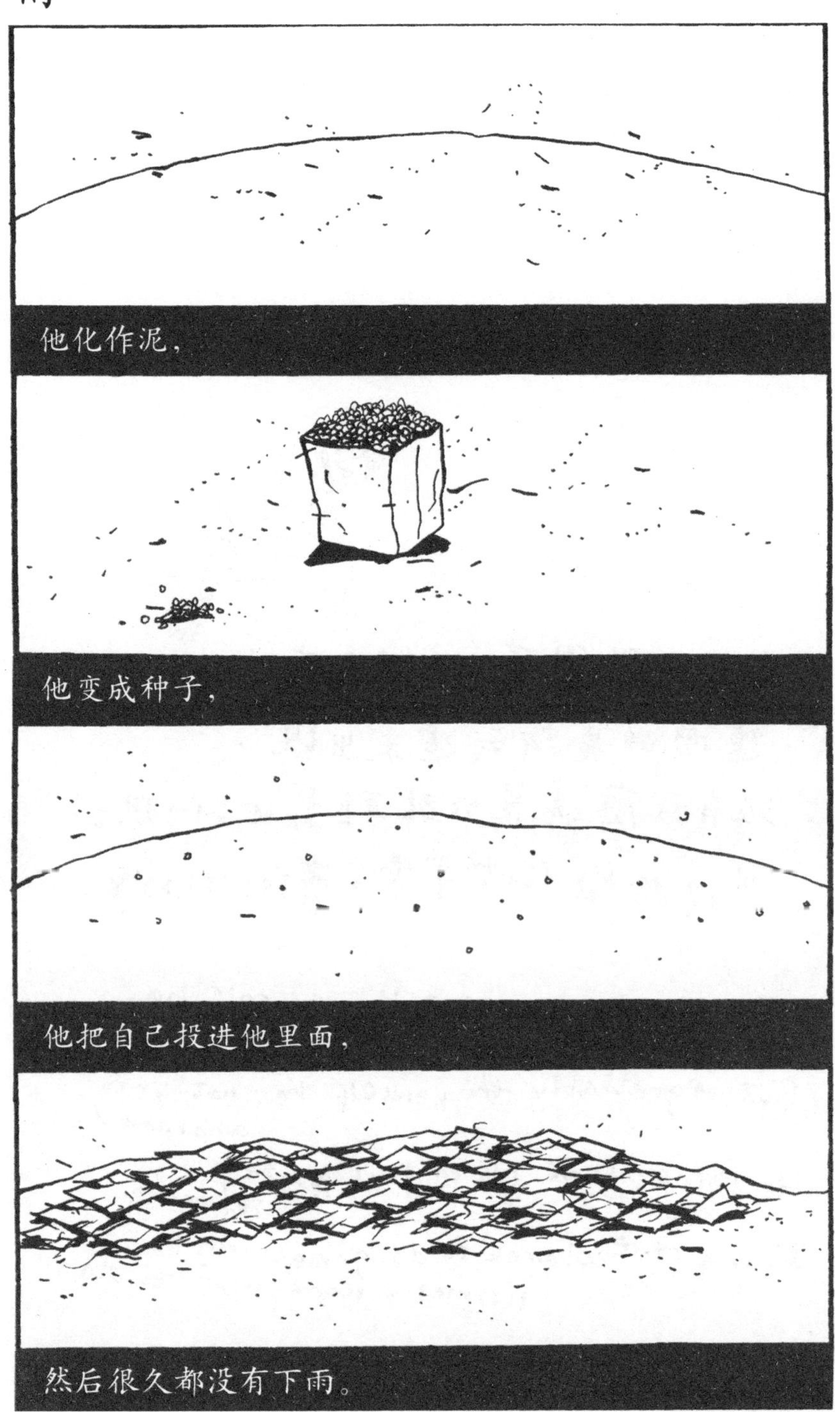

我
Self

有一天他發覺舊我已經死去，
遺憾的是新我還未出現，
沒有我應該是比較輕鬆吧，他想。
可得趁機做些平常不應該做的事。

One day he finds that the old self has already died.
But regrettably the new self has not yet appeared.
He thinks that No self is quite relaxing.
It is a rare chance to do something he normally dares not to do.

我

情事

Love Affairs

從來相信一見鍾情
追追逐逐是難免的事．
確定就是他就一定要把他捉到手，
自然也有方法把他留下來

I have always believed in love at first sight.
It definitely involoves some chasing around.
Hold fast onto him if you are sure it's him
Naturally, there's some way to keep him.

情事

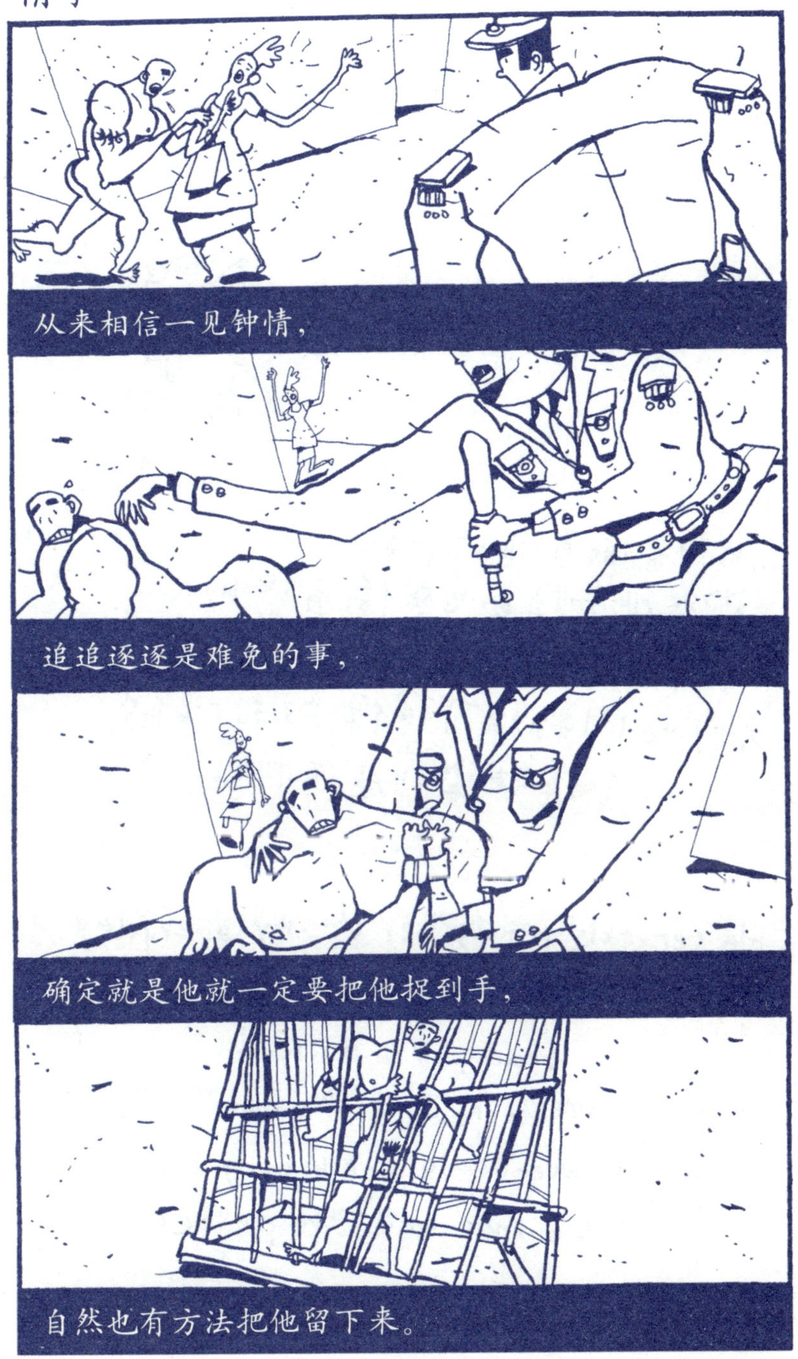

日記

Diary

他每天偷看她的日記

當然他知道她也在偷看他的。

他/她們就這樣更深入的了解對方，

他/她們終於可以像公主和王子般

永遠快樂的生活下去。

He secretly reads her diary everyday

He certainly knows that she secretly reads his as well.

So they come to know each other more this way

And they eventually live happily ever after like the prince and the princess.

日记

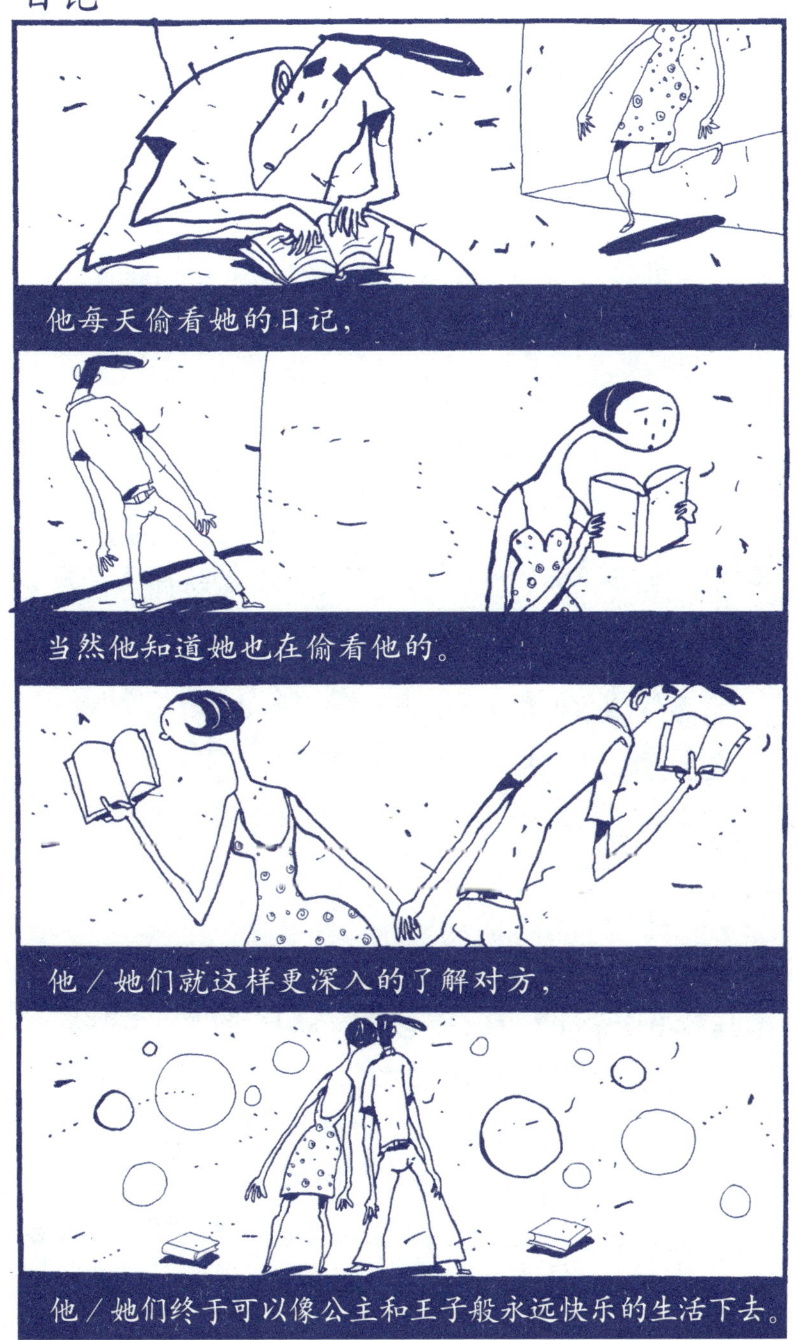
他每天偷看她的日记，
当然他知道她也在偷看他的。
他／她们就这样更深入的了解对方，
他／她们终于可以像公主和王子般永远快乐的生活下去。

這一個夜
Tonight

既不浪漫綺旎又不浴血火爆的一晚是多麼珍貴，
電視太好看於是他/她們懶得開口，
坐着坐着他/她們的婚姻有了新意義，
從前是這樣日後也會如此永恒。

It's very rare to have a night
that is not romantic or violent.
Watching TV is so enjoyable that they
don't want to talk.
New meaning evolves in their marriage
as they sit and watch.
It was like this, and will be like this forever

这一个夜

既不浪漫旖旎又不浴血火爆的一晚是多么珍贵，
电视太好看于是他/她们懒得开口，
坐着坐着他/她们的婚姻有了新意义，
从前是这样日后也会如此永恒。

8990勾留台北一年，
不同的生活环境和经验碰撞刺激出《我的天》漫画系列的创作，
及后数年，完成了上千则四格故事，
于台北编辑结集四本《我的天》。
另有香港、内地、日本几个不同版本。

这本真是很奇怪的书！
这本书能令读者自由出入于文字与图画，中英文之间，
实在是个难得的经验，喜欢漫画或文字的人都不难发现其可读之处。

—— 潘启迪《不是漫画的漫画》

白的面，蓝的底，是天是地是海是云是想像。
四格漫画盛载的原来可以这样多。载的是人气。
满满的，没有完整的故事，细琢的画工，
一个人物，一件小事，一个情景，一份感觉，就自自然然地展开了。
想阿霖早已有自己一套说情说事的方法（语言？），
没有咄咄逼人的霸气，
没有知识分子的自觉，却是柔柔淡淡的，最终都是给余地和空间。

—— 俞若玫《天空这样大》

他的四格漫画不谈政治，不搞好笑，更不是幽默讽刺，而是一种感觉，
像沉伏在城市尘埃落净之后，月白风清，寂然无声的一个画面，
你对着四格漫画，是四格镜子，
照到自己的心，朋友的心，生活的心和梦想的心。

—— 林超荣《我的天》

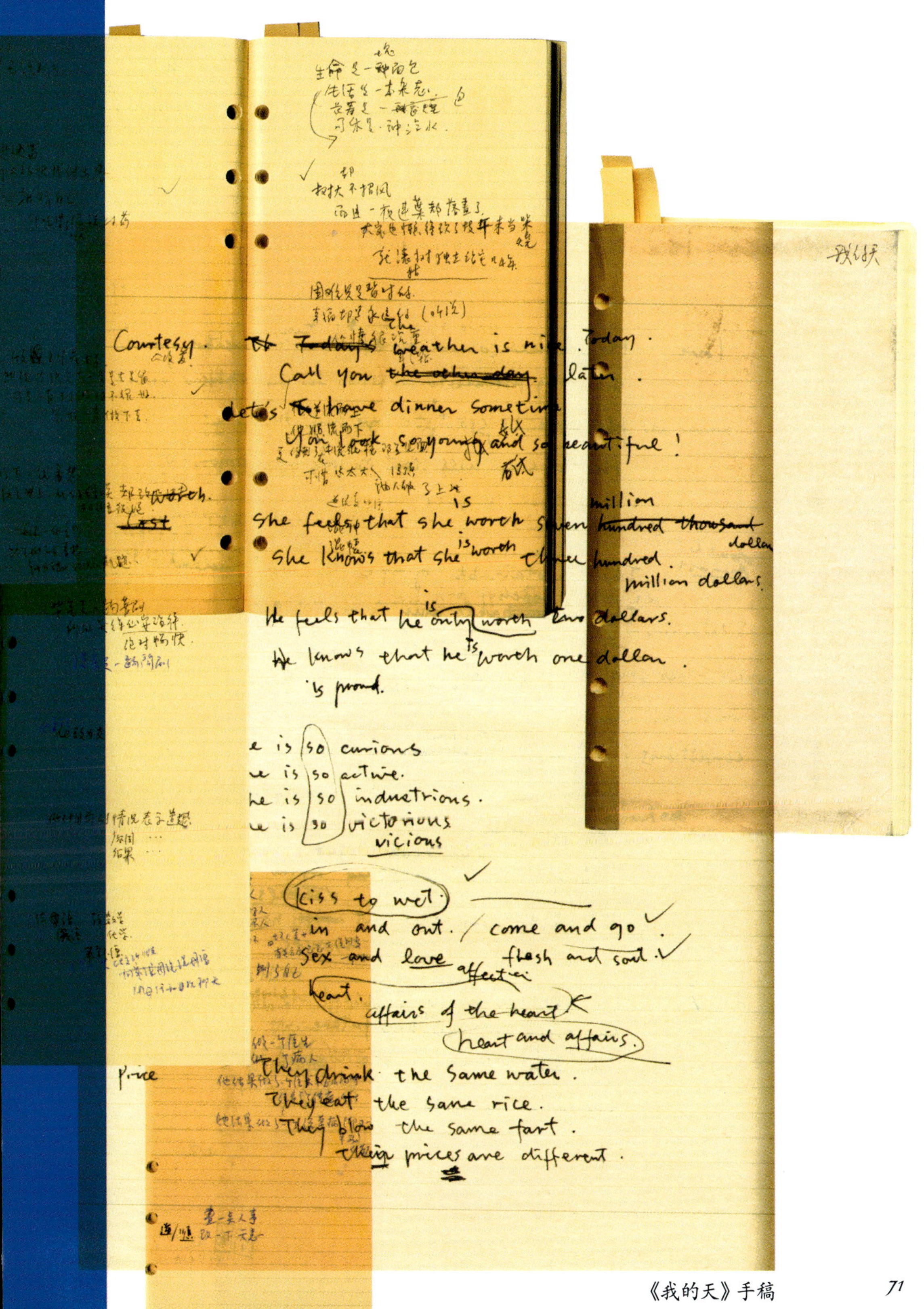

《我的天》手稿

香港《经济日报》《我的天》漫画连载（九六年）

台北《中时晚报》
《我的天》漫画连载（九〇—九三年）

台北《中国时报》漫画连载
《我的天》前身《世纪末游乐》（八九—九〇年）

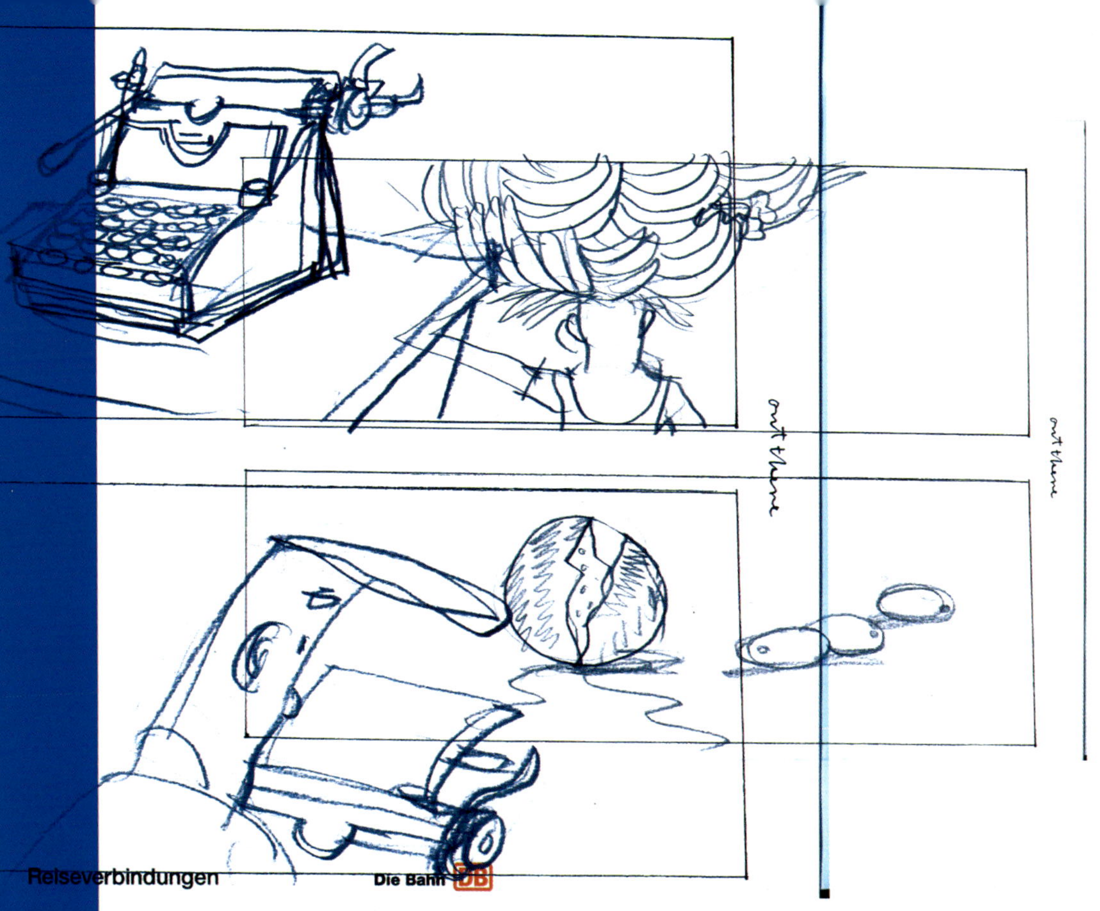

out there
out there
Reiseverbindungen
Die Bahn DB
se Reiseverbindungen bei Fahrscheinkauf bzw. Platzreservierung vor, damit Ihre Reiseunterlagen
m Reiseweg erstellt werden können. Nähere Informationen erhalten Sie in DB ReiseZentren, beim
Bahn (Tel: 01805-99 66 33, gebührenpflichtig), in Reisebüros mit DB-Lizenz sowie unter www.bahn.de.
en Abschluss eines persönlichen Reiseschutzes und wünschen Ihnen eine angenehme Reise.
(Main)Hbf
ELLE UHR GLEIS ZUG BEMERKUNG
)Hbf ab 09:15 7 ICE 694 a)
Garten an 13:19 1
Sie mögliche Gleisänderungen vor Ort !
auer: 4:04, täglich
einfache Fahrt (ohne Ermäßigung);
F*GOE*SDI*R)
DBAG
ONNN
nt
rankfurt (Main)Hbf
08.01,07:19 K07742
Sie Kodak Bilder. Ihre Reise-Erinnerungen sind es wert!

《我的天》草稿

《我的天》香港版（九五年）

《我的天》台湾版（九七—九八年）

《我的天》内地版（九八年）

MUSCLE MAN
01
LUCY
OFFICE LADY

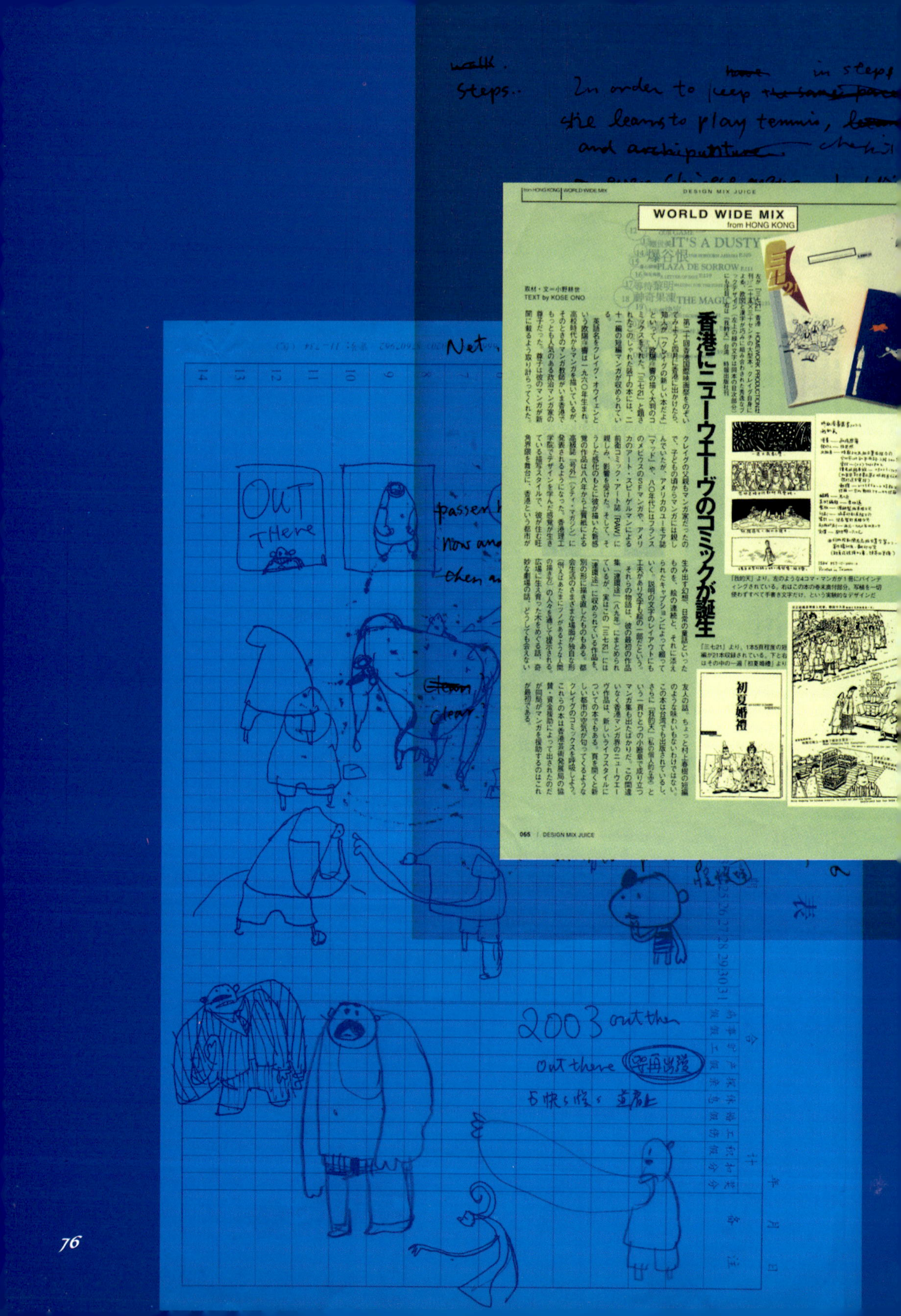

steps.. In order to keep

she learns to play tennis,

and acupuncture

WORLD WIDE MIX
from HONG KONG

香港にニューウエーヴのコミックが誕生

取材・文＝小野耕世
TEXT by KOSE ONO

第二十回香港国際映画祭をのぞいてみようと四月に香港に出かけたら、知人が「クレイグの新しい本だよ」といって、欧陽應霽の描く大判のコミックスをくれた。「三七21」と題されたこのしゃれた装丁の本には、二十一編の短編マンガが収められている。

英語名をクレイグ・オウイェンという欧陽應霽は一九六〇年生まれ。高校時代からマンガを描いているが、そのときのマンガ教師がいま香港でもっとも人気のある政治マンガ家の尊子だった。尊子は彼のマンガが新聞に載るよう取り計らってくれた。

クレイグの父親もマンガ家だったので、子どもの頃からマンガには親しんでいたが、アメリカのユーモア誌「マッド」や、八〇年代にはフランスのメビウスのSFマンガや、アメリカのアート・スピーゲルマンによる前衛コミック・アート誌「RAW」に親しみ、影響を受けた。そして、そうした感化のもとに彼が描いた新感覚の作品は八八年から上質紙による高級誌「號外」（シティ・マガジン）に発表されるようになった。香港理工学院でデザインを学んだ感覚が生きている描写スタイルで、彼が住む旺角界隈を舞台に、香港という都市が生み出す幻想、日常の童話といったものを、絵の連続と、それに添えられたキャプションによって綴っていく。説明の文字のレイアウトにも工夫があり文字も絵の一部だという。

それらの物語は、彼の最初の作品集「逮頭送」（八九年）にまとめられているが、実はこの「三七21」には「逮頭送」に収められている作品を、別の形に描き直したものもある。都会生活のさまざまな場面が独自な形（例えばあたまにツノがあるような人間の描き方）の人々を通して提示される。広場に生え育った木をめぐる話、奇妙な劇場の話、どうしても会えない友人の話。ちょっと村上春樹の短編のような味わいもないわけではない。この本は台湾でも出版されているし、さらに「我的天」（私の個人的な空）という一頁ひとつの小断章で成り立つマンガ集も出たばかりだ。この間違いなく香港マンガ界のニューウエーヴ作品は、新しいライフスタイルについての本でもある。頁を開くと新しい都市の空気が匂ってくるようなクレイグのコミックスを詳説しよう。これらの本は香港芸術発展局の協賛・資金援助によって出されたのだが同局がマンガを援助するのはこれが最初である。

左が「三七21」香港 HOMEWORK PRODUCTION社刊 二十六×三十センチの大判本。クレイグ自身による、欧陽と漢字が巧みに組み合わされた洒落なブックデザイン（左上の線の文字は同本の目次部分）右は「我的天」台湾 時報出版社刊

「我的天」より。左のような4コマ・マンガが1冊にバインディングされている。右はこの本の巻末奥付部分。写植を一切使わずすべて手書き文字だけ、という実験的なデザインだ

「三七21」より。1本5頁程度の短編が21本収録されている。下と右はその中の一遍「初夏婚禮」より

初夏婚禮

《我的天》日本版（○二年）

《我的天》展览（○○年东京）

制服男
Monster from Space
Monster From Earth
行動藝術家
/搬運工友
肌肉男
DJ
Ma Ma Mia
OL Slave
Big Brother Boss
Wanderer

在应霁的漫画里，没有美和丑。追求美丑只会落得一片空白和迷惘。

在这个漫画角度里，也没有平衡和工整。
五官只是符号，手脚只是没意义的形状。
我们反而会记得暗无天日的地下铁、巨大的仙人掌、长角的人头、外星人。
没有爱情，没有感情，毫无生气，只有意识在飘流。

解读应霁，跟解读他的漫画，可以是两回事。
看过他照片的人，有一阵惊喜，
惊是在于他的神采，和图像的意识形态，那么割裂。
喜是在于他没有丝毫漫画家沦落的日子。
人和漫画血肉相连，有时是吃力的一回事。

看应霁的文字，是一种修为，思绪完全要经过反刍，才理出个头绪来。
看应霁的漫画，是更大的修炼，
是对头脑逻辑思想的一个磨练，弄得不好，脑部神经会严重受损。

——马露媛　九六年一月

当香港的欧阳应霁四格漫画第一次出现在台湾的报纸上，
读者都惊叹于作者透过四格漫画呈现洞察世事般的人生风景，
原本只是搞笑的四格漫画，对欧阳应霁来说，却成了一项新游戏，
运用这个游戏，记录日常生活的荒谬与无力，生命的惊世骇俗！

这本书像是欧阳的日记，
记录他每天都要做的事情，每天给自己不同的定位，不停转换的身份。
他说他自己是一个对于新鲜事物都充满好奇的人，
思想随时处在一个流动的状态，还贪心地将它们记录在自己的作品里面，
并不担心是不是大家都能接受。
因为读者是可以被培养出来的，而不是一味地依着大众的喜好
给他们棒棒糖吃，酸梅也不错，苦瓜也不错。

——王信智　〇〇年九月

聽說
I was Told….

聽說兩個男人之間的愛沒有好結果，
聽說不同年紀的愛也很難長久，
聽說一吻就會有愛滋，
聽說吃太多巧克力會胖。

I was told that Love between two men
would never come to anything.
I was told that Love between people with
age difference would never last.
I was told that AIDS could be contracted
through a kiss.
I was told that one would get fat
eating too much chocolate.

听说

咒

Curse

他強迫她說愛他，
她想想說說也無妨也就輕易的說了。
可是她不曉得這是個原則問題，
從此以後她就空着嘴巴
再說不出一句話。

He forces her to tell him that she loves him
She thinks it's no big deal and thus
she tells him so carelessly.
She does not realise that it is a matter of
principle.
From then onwards, she could speak no more.

咒

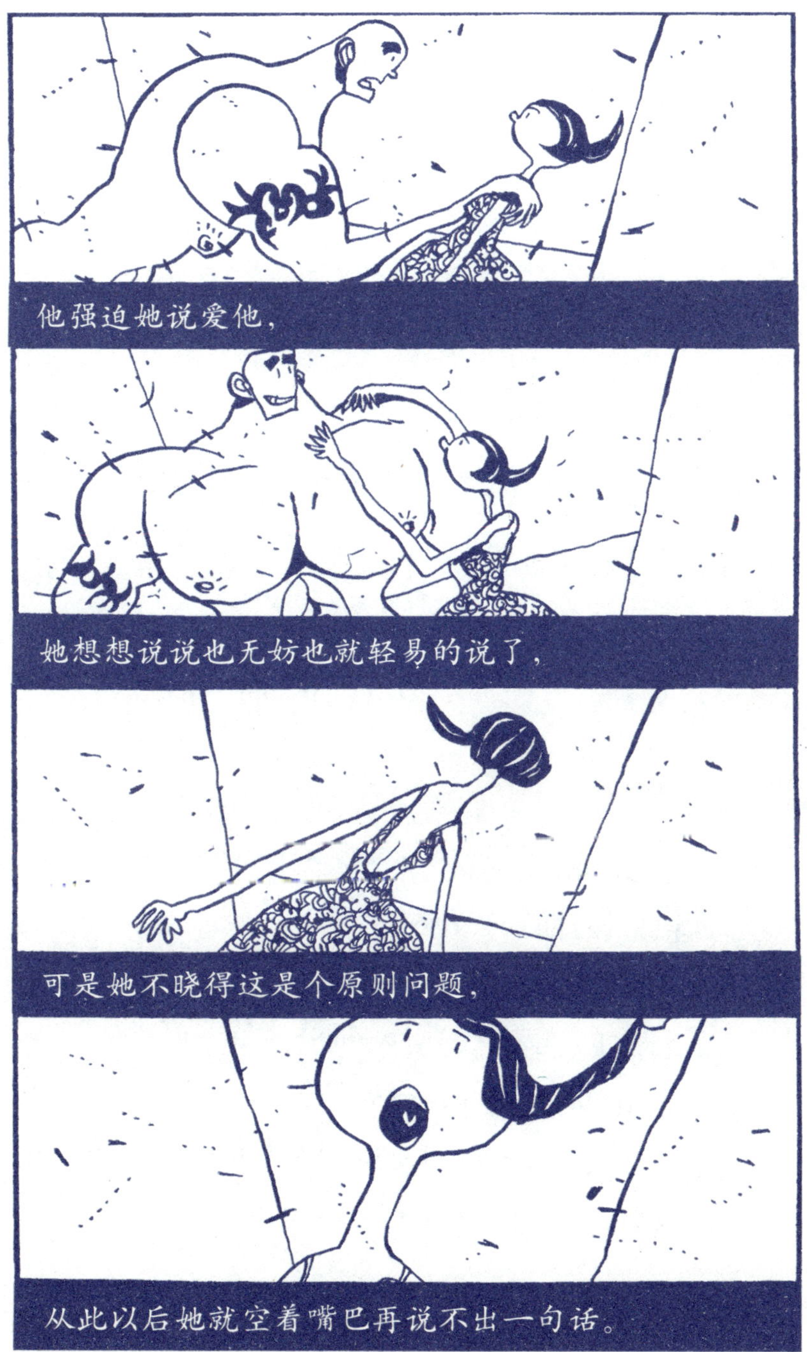
他强迫她说爱他，
她想想说说也无妨也就轻易的说了，
可是她不晓得这是个原则问题，
从此以后她就空着嘴巴再说不出一句话。

最新戀情
The Latest Romance

為了了解他 他得熟讀使用手冊十數次，
為了關係一直可以繼續，他得準備充足的電，
只要不生銹，愛就可以永恒，
只要勤換顏色，感覺就可以永遠新鮮。

In order to understand him, he studies the manual many times.
In order to make the relationship last,
he stocks up substantial energy.
Love will last forever as long as it doesn't rust.
Feeling of freshness could be maintained
if colours could be changed regularly

最新不了情

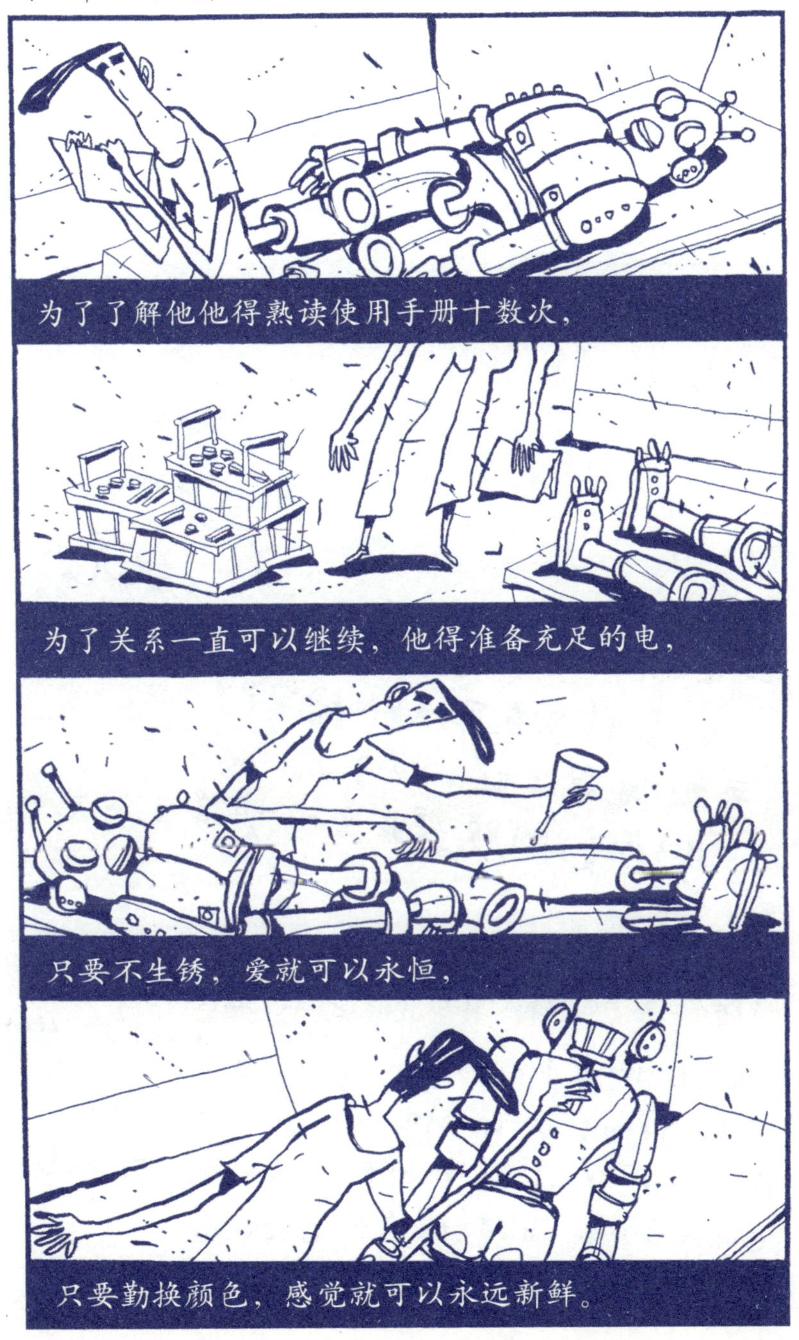
为了了解他他得熟读使用手册十数次，
为了关系一直可以继续，他得准备充足的电，
只要不生锈，爱就可以永恒，
只要勤换颜色，感觉就可以永远新鲜。

原則

Principle

二十多年的爭吵還是沒完沒了

到最後只有再次離開家門。

看來這是最後的一次了。

為了原則問題還是要把想罵的罵完。

There's no end to their dispute for the last 20 years

Got to leave home again after all.

It seems it would be the last time.

As a matter of principle, she has to get everything out of her chest.

原则

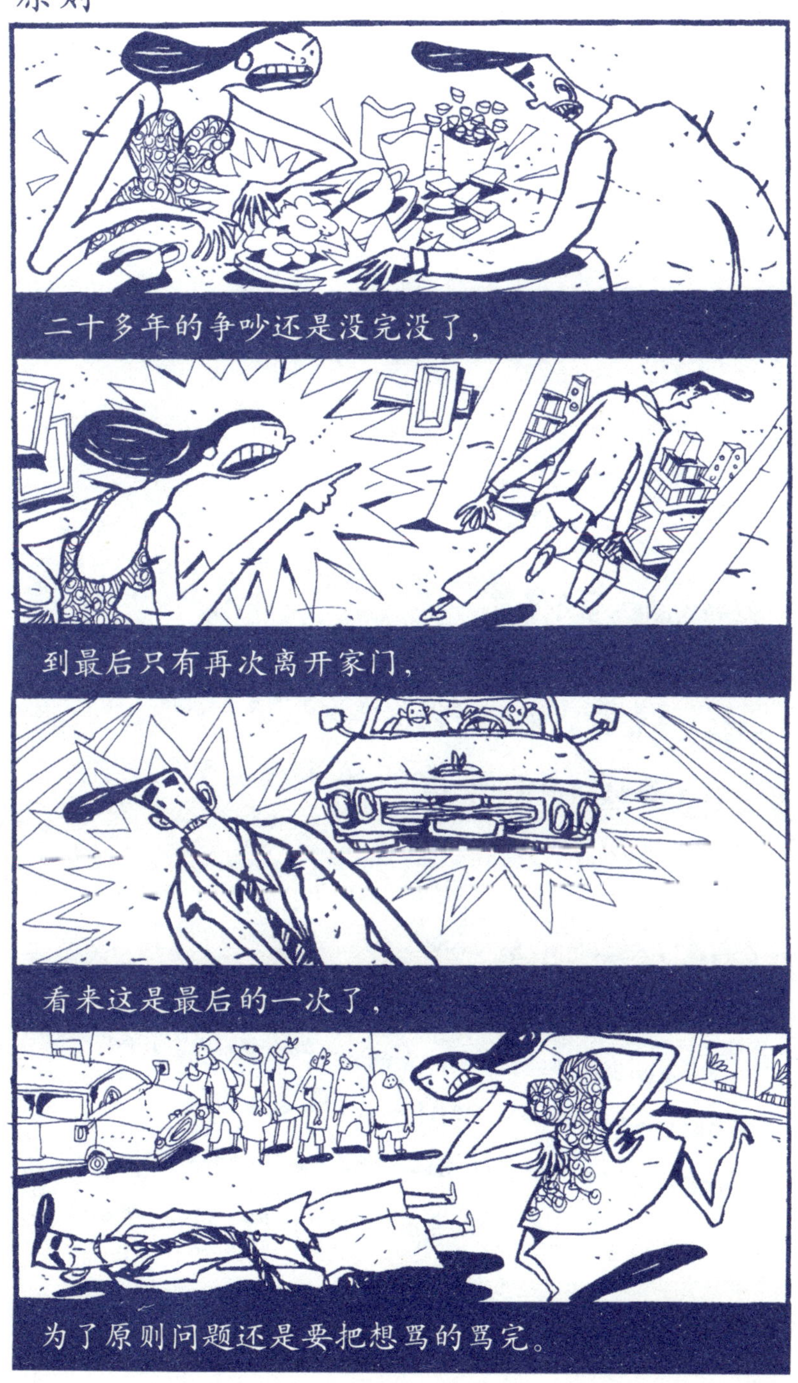

思想起

Remember

坐在他的車裡，

他說起她。

至於遠方的他和再不會出現的她，

因為車速太快也真的有點模糊了。

Sitting in his car,

He remembers her

He remembers him from faraway, and her

whom he would nener meet again

Everything gets blurred because of

the speeding of the car

思想起

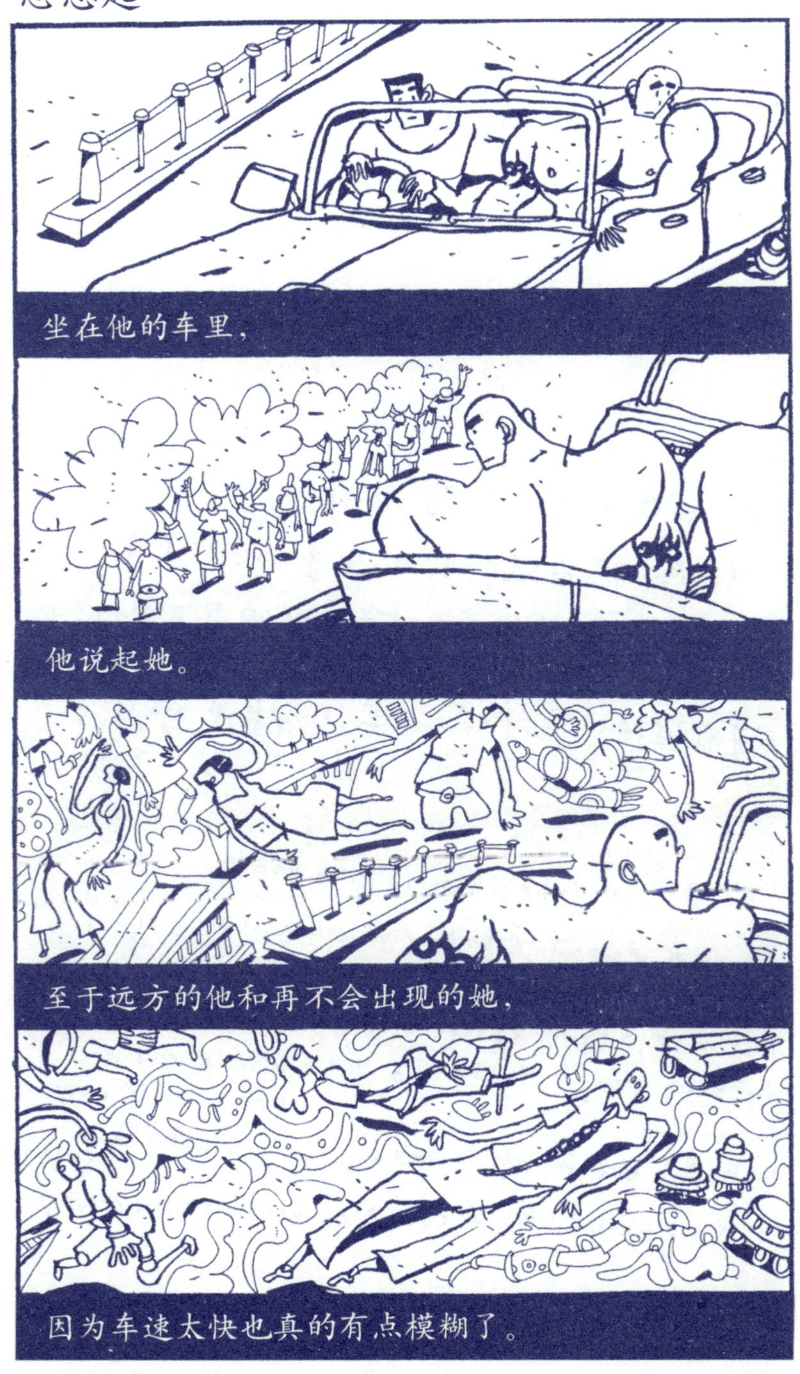

沙灘的一天

A Day On the Beach.

爸爸帶他到沙灘堆沙，
作為一個有建設性的兒童，他絕不馬虎，
沙堡堆好了，父子倆才驚覺浪是不會打到這邊來，
沒有浪把沙堡沖塌，堆沙有甚麼樂趣和意義？

His father takes him to the beach.
Being a creative and constructive child,
he works seriously.
After the sand castle is built, they realise
to their surprise that no wave would ever
come this way.
What's the meaning and fun of building sand castle
if no wave would come to wash them away.

沙滩的一天

爸爸带他到沙滩堆沙，
作为一个有建设性的儿童，他绝不马虎，
沙堡堆好了，父子俩才惊觉浪是不会打到这边来，
没有浪把沙堡冲塌，堆沙有什么乐趣和意义？

遺囑

The Will

她決定要立下遺囑。
她打算把爸爸留給漂亮的班主任林老師，
把一大堆做不完的功課留給同班的討厭的李小強。
把她暗戀的黃志明永遠留在遊樂場。

She decides to make a will.
She is planning to leave her father
to the beautiful teacher, Miss Lam.
To leave her pile of never-ending homework
to that despicable classmate Johnny Lee,
And to leave Anthony Wong, the one she secretly admires, in the amusement park forever.

遗嘱

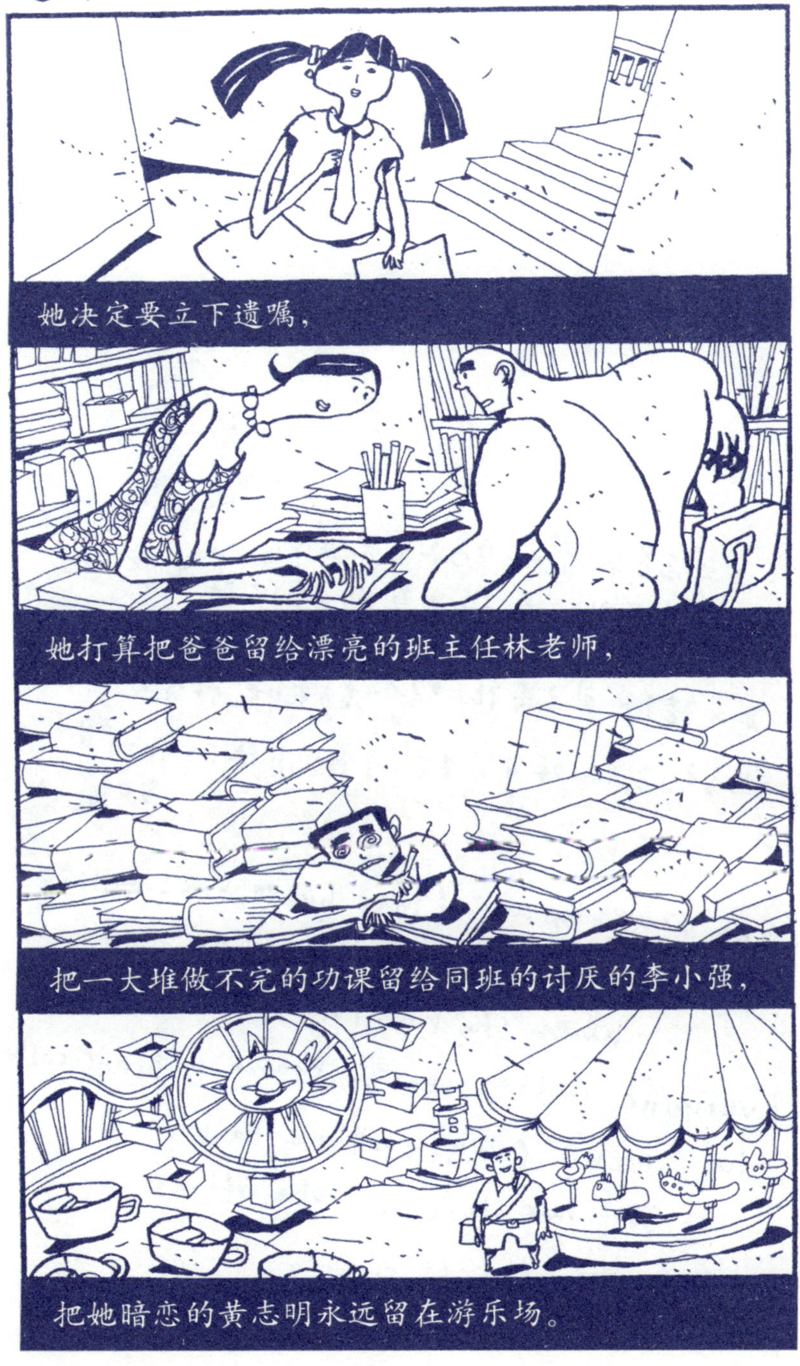

她决定要立下遗嘱，
她打算把爸爸留给漂亮的班主任林老师，
把一大堆做不完的功课留给同班的讨厌的李小强，
把她暗恋的黄志明永远留在游乐场。

得失記
Lost and Found

一覺醒來覺得自己不再完整，
她決定要努力記起是甚麼時候在甚麼地方
丟掉的，
走上街只見滿街的人都在慌忙尋覓——
她終於在辦公室找到自己遺落的那一根
頭髮。

She wakes up and finds herself incomplete.
She tries very hard to remember
when she has lost it.
Everyone in the street is searching frantically,
she finally finds that one hair
she has lost in the office.

得失记

一觉醒来觉得自己不再完整，
她决定要努力记起是什么时候在什么地方丢掉的，
走上街只见满街的人都在慌忙寻觅——
她终于在办公室找到自己遗落的那一根头发。

行李
Luggage

一不小心又把行李弄丟了，
四處找行李之際竟然找着要找的人，
一心一意跟他回家開始新生活，
一進門滿眼是他撿回來的行李。

Not paying attention, she loses her luggage.
She finds him, the one she's been waiting
for while looking for the luggage.
Without hesitation, she follows him home
to start a new life.
As she enters the house, she sees lying
in front of her all the luggage he has
picked up.

行李

一不小心又把行李弄丢了，
四处找行李之际竟然找着要找的人，
一心一意跟他回家开始新生活；
一进门满眼是他捡回来的行李。

困

Trapped

三天以来已經被困在電梯五次，
悶起来只好自己發明一些可以數的小動物。
希望這是幸運的第六次被困經驗。
到了八樓他好端端的走出去。

It's the 5th time she has been trapped
inside the elevator in 3 days.
It's so boring that she starts to invent
some small animals for counting.
She wishes that this would be the lucky 6th time.
He walks out with no problem on the 8th floor.

困

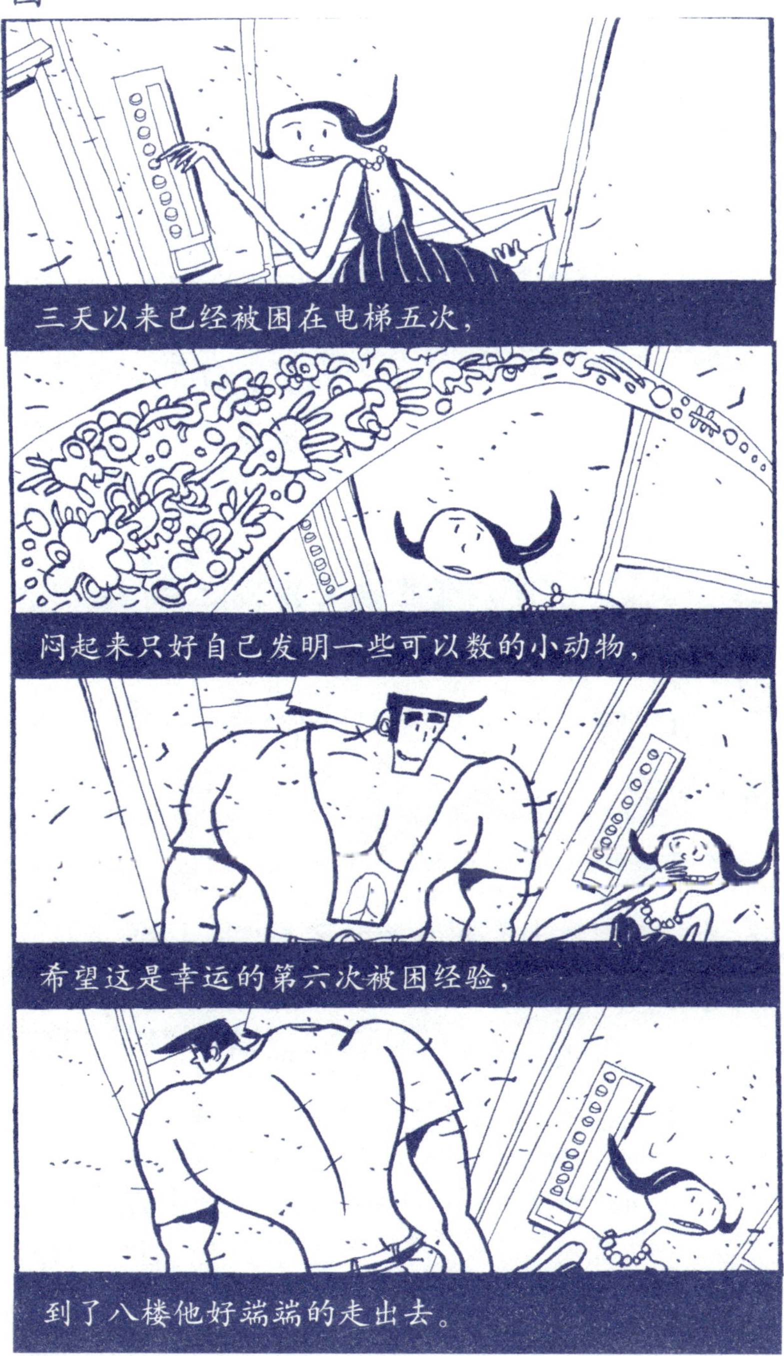
三天以来已经被困在电梯五次，
闷起来只好自己发明一些可以数的小动物，
希望这是幸运的第六次被困经验，
到了八楼他好端端的走出去。

鮮花和鮮血

Flowers and Blood

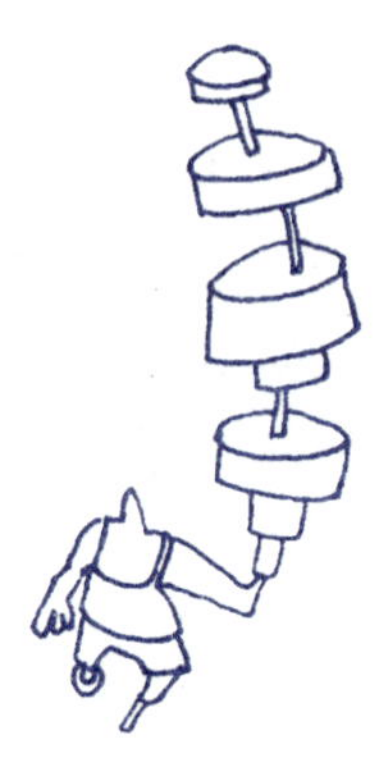

種了十年的好看的花突然一夜間死光了.
她開始懷疑大自然在遺棄她.
一個渺小的人究竟可以做甚麽呢?
她開始吃二分熟的帶血的牛排。

All the beautiful flowers she has nurtured
for ten years die suddenly overnight.
She begins to think that nature has forsaken her
What could an insignificant person like herself do?
She begins to eat her beef raw and bloody.

鲜花和鲜血

种了十年的好看的花突然一夜间死光了，
她开始怀疑大自然在遗弃她。
一个渺小的人究竟可以做什么呢？
她开始吃二分熟的带血的牛排。

煙火夜

The Night of the Fireworks

一夜天花亂墜，
忽明忽暗中他對她說愛她。
熱鬧過後人潮如水退去，
獨自回家的路上她口渴想喝一瓶可樂。

The fireworks are beautiful tonight.
He tells her he love her vaguely and ambiguously.
people scatter and disappear after the joy and Laughter.
She wants a coke to quench her thirst as she walks home alone.

烟火夜

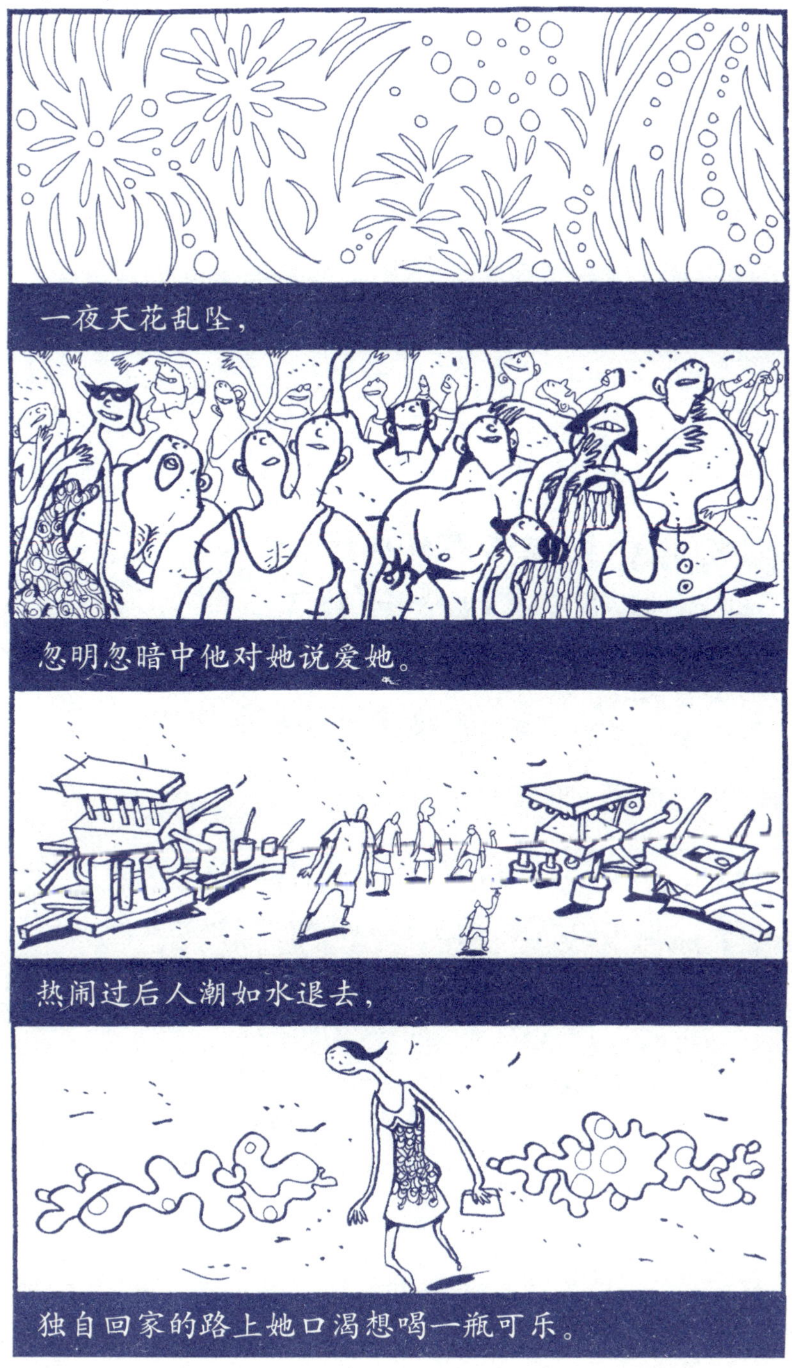

信

letter

他寫好了一封信到郵局裡要寄出．
郵局職員有禮貌的拒絕了．
原因是信裡負載了太多的期盼、責任和熱情，
恐怕目前的郵遞服務不勝負荷。

He takes a letter he wrote to the Post office
The man behind the counter refuses politely
to take the letter,
Because the letter is too heavy with expectations,
responsibilities and passions.
Lest that it would be too much for
the existing postal service.

信

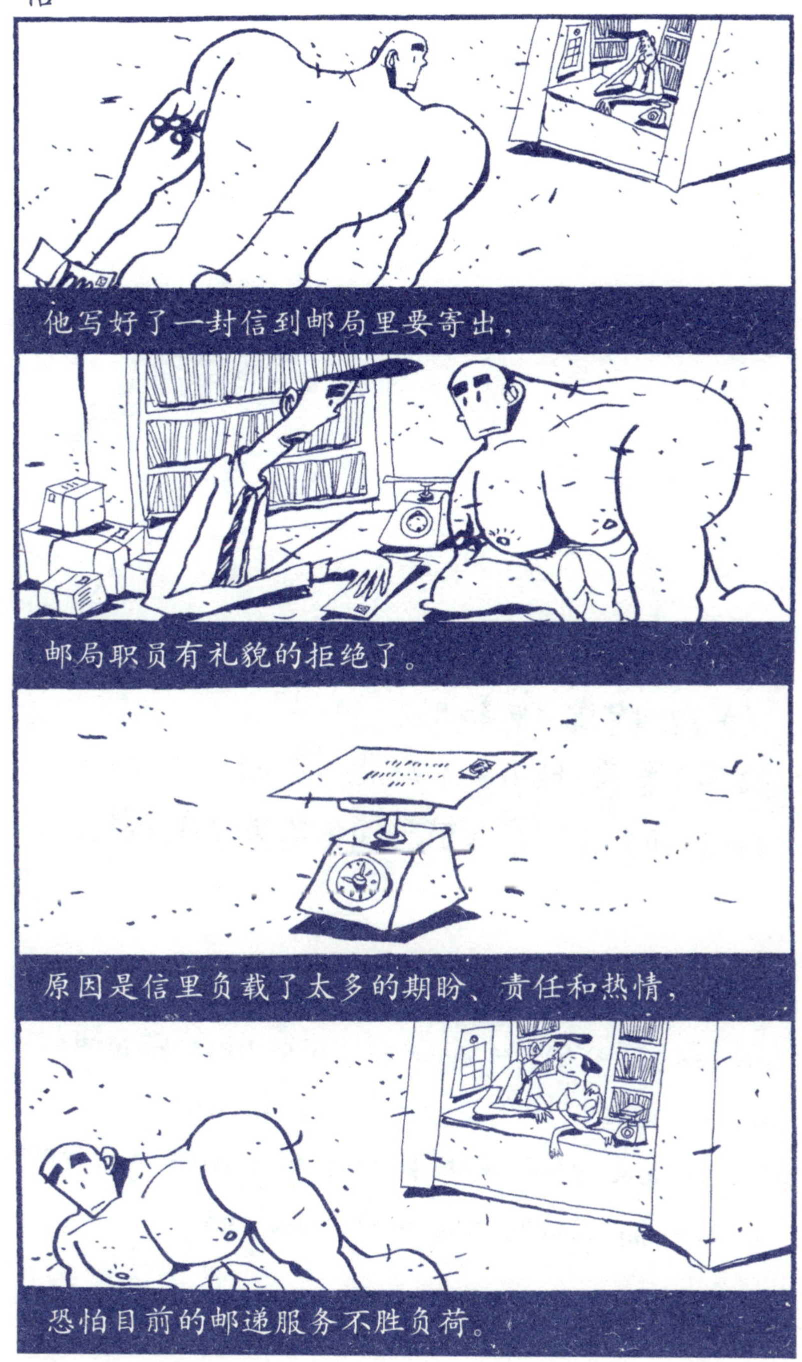
他写好了一封信到邮局里要寄出，
邮局职员有礼貌的拒绝了。
原因是信里负载了太多的期盼、责任和热情，
恐怕目前的邮递服务不胜负荷。

水果先生

MR. Fruits

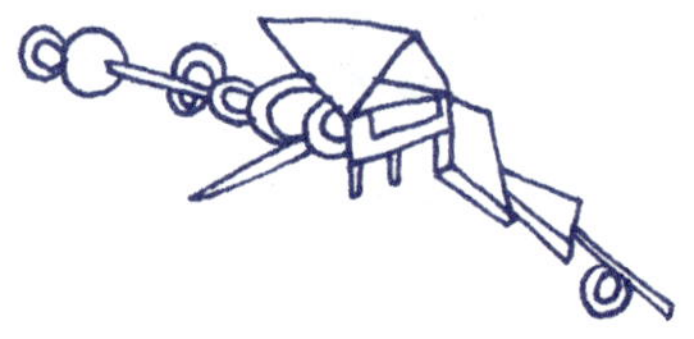

他是如此的信任蘋果

他把橙當作知己，

沒有了香蕉的日子不知怎麼過？

他和西瓜約會之際又怕芒果不高興。

He trusts the apples completely.

He considers the oranges his best friends.

He couldn't live without the bananas.

He's afraid that the mangoes would get upset

if he dates the watermelons.

水果先生

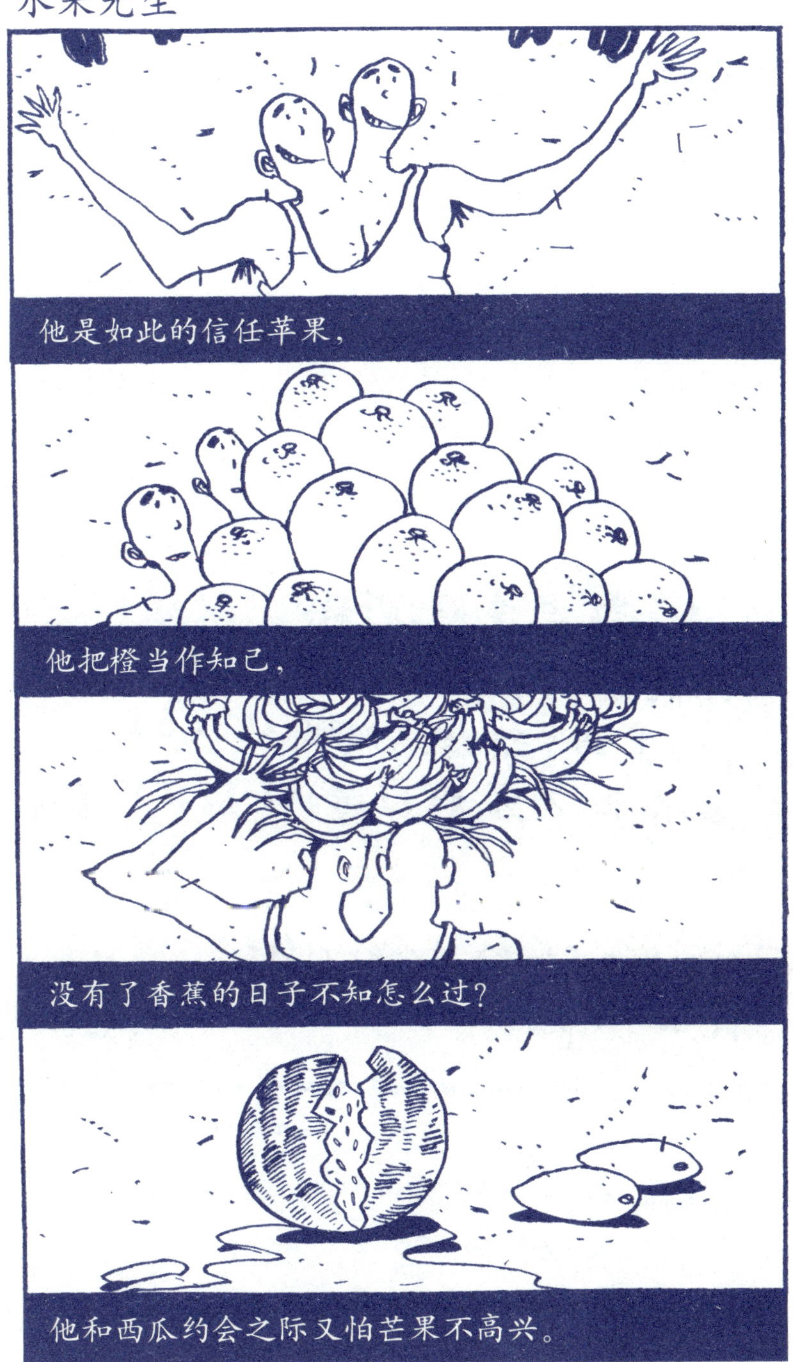

另一種情書
Love Letter of Another Kind

這是一部偷來的打字機，
功能良好，只有一個小小的缺點。
打出來的字都沒法在字典裡找到
他嘀嘀嗒嗒地打一封信給他的愛人。

This is a stolen typewriter
It works perfectly with only one minor fault.
All the words typed out could not be found in a dictionary.
Pounding on his typewriter, he types out a letter to his lover

另一种情书

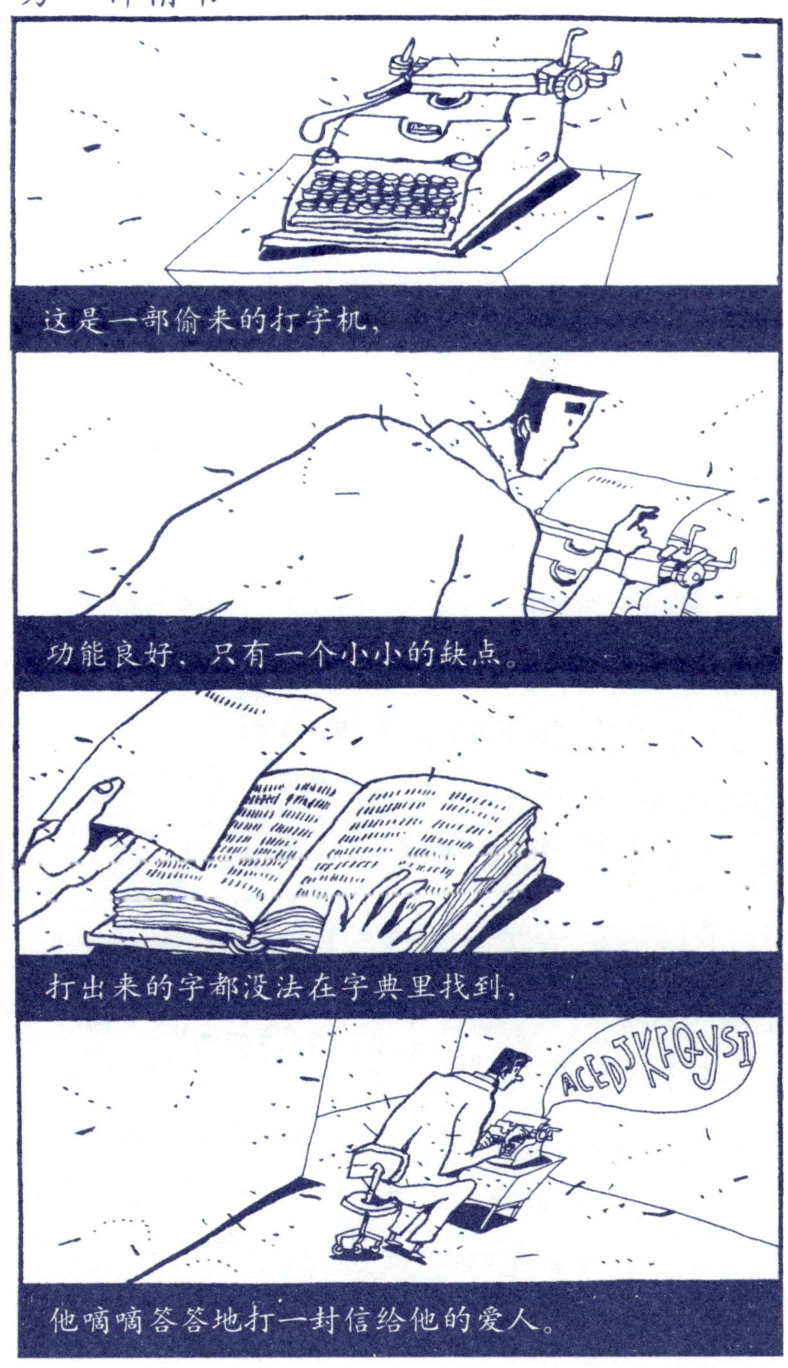
这是一部偷来的打字机，
功能良好，只有一个小小的缺点。
打出来的字都没法在字典里找到，
ACEDJKFQYSI
他嘀嘀答答地打一封信给他的爱人。

貓或沙發

The Cat And The Sofa

他有一隻心愛的貓，
他有一張新買的意大利沙發。
他的貓把他的沙發的漂亮的表面抓破了，
他究竟是應該把貓丟掉或者把沙發丟掉？

He loves his cat,
He loves the new sofa he bought from Italy.
His cat tears his sofa with scratches.
He doesn't know if he should throw away his cat or his sofa.

猫或沙发

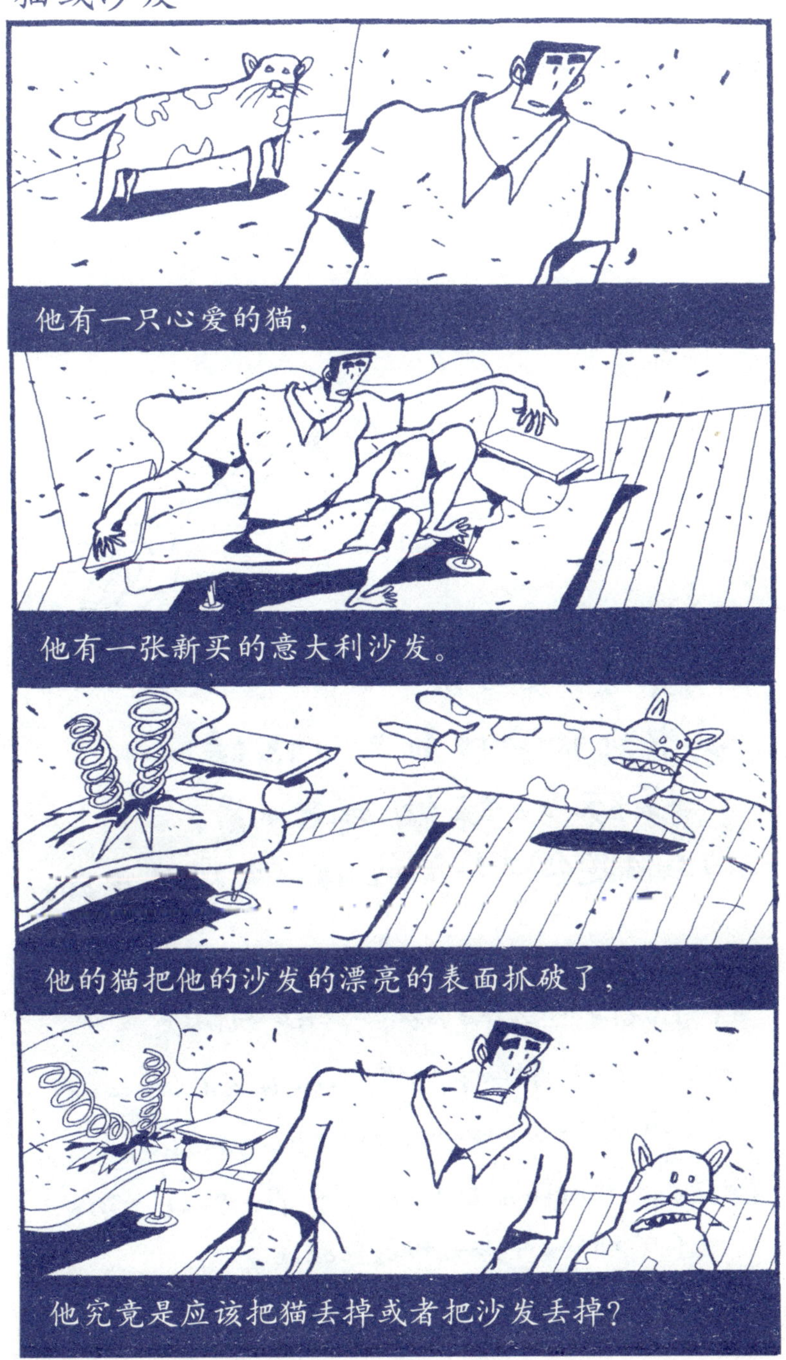
他有一只心爱的猫，
他有一张新买的意大利沙发。
他的猫把他的沙发的漂亮的表面抓破了，
他究竟是应该把猫丢掉或者把沙发丢掉？

恐龍与螞蟻

The Dinosaur And The Ants

如果他是一隻恐龍，他想，
他一定把那滿地亂跑的螞蟻——
踩踩踩踩個稀巴爛，
因為在這個大社會裡根本容不下小東西。

"If I were a dinosaur," he thinks.
He would stamp and crush all the ants.
that run around on the ground
Because there's no place for such tiny
creatures in this society.

恐龙与蚂蚁

鐵甲老人

MR. Old Robot

當年為了保護地球，
他不惜犧牲了右臂和左腳，
可惜如今鮮有人記得他的豐功偉績，
過馬路的時候也沒有小朋友樂意扶他一把。

In order to protect the Earth,
He had sacrificed his right arm and his left foot.
It's a pity that nobody remembers him and his accomplishments today.
Not a single person, not even a child would help him cross the road now.

铁甲老人

当年为了保护地球，
他不惜牺牲了右臂和左脚，
可惜如今鲜有人记得他的丰功伟绩，
过马路的时候也没有小朋友乐意扶他一把。

等

Wait

妝化好了，裙穿好了，耳環帶好了，攝影師到了
菲林裝上了，燈光打好了。
音樂夠響了，姿勢夠美了，笑容夠燦爛了，
大家在等。
在等一片或者會飄過的雲。

The hair is set, The earrings are set.
The set is set. The cameras are set.
The films are set. The Lights are set.
The music is right, The postures are right.
The smiles are right.
Everybody is waiting,
Waiting for the piece of cloud that might pass by.

等

妆化好了，裙穿好了，耳环带好了，
摄影师到了，菲林装上了，灯光打好了，

音乐够响了，姿势够美了，笑容够灿烂了，

大家在等，

在等一片或者会飘过的云。

天外來

From Outer space

在毫無心理準備之下給他碰見它.
多看幾眼也實在不外如是.
久而久之大家都習以為常且開始批評
其款式過時.
還是標奇立異的會為大家帶來多一點刺激。

It took him by surprise
It's nothing much after a few encounters.
After a while, people started to
criticise its look.
Only the strange and outlandish
would never fail to excite people.

天外来

在毫无心理准备之下给他碰见它，
多看几眼也实在不外如是，
久而久之大家都习以为常且开始批评其款式过时，
还是标奇立异的会为大家带来多一点刺激。

問題

Problem

縱是萬分不願意,
時限已到,終於要被接回去。
可能是傳送机器出了點小問題——
問題是以後該怎么辦?

Though it is very much against her will,
the time is up, she has to be transmitted back.
But there is a malfunction with the transmitter
Though it creates problems.

问题

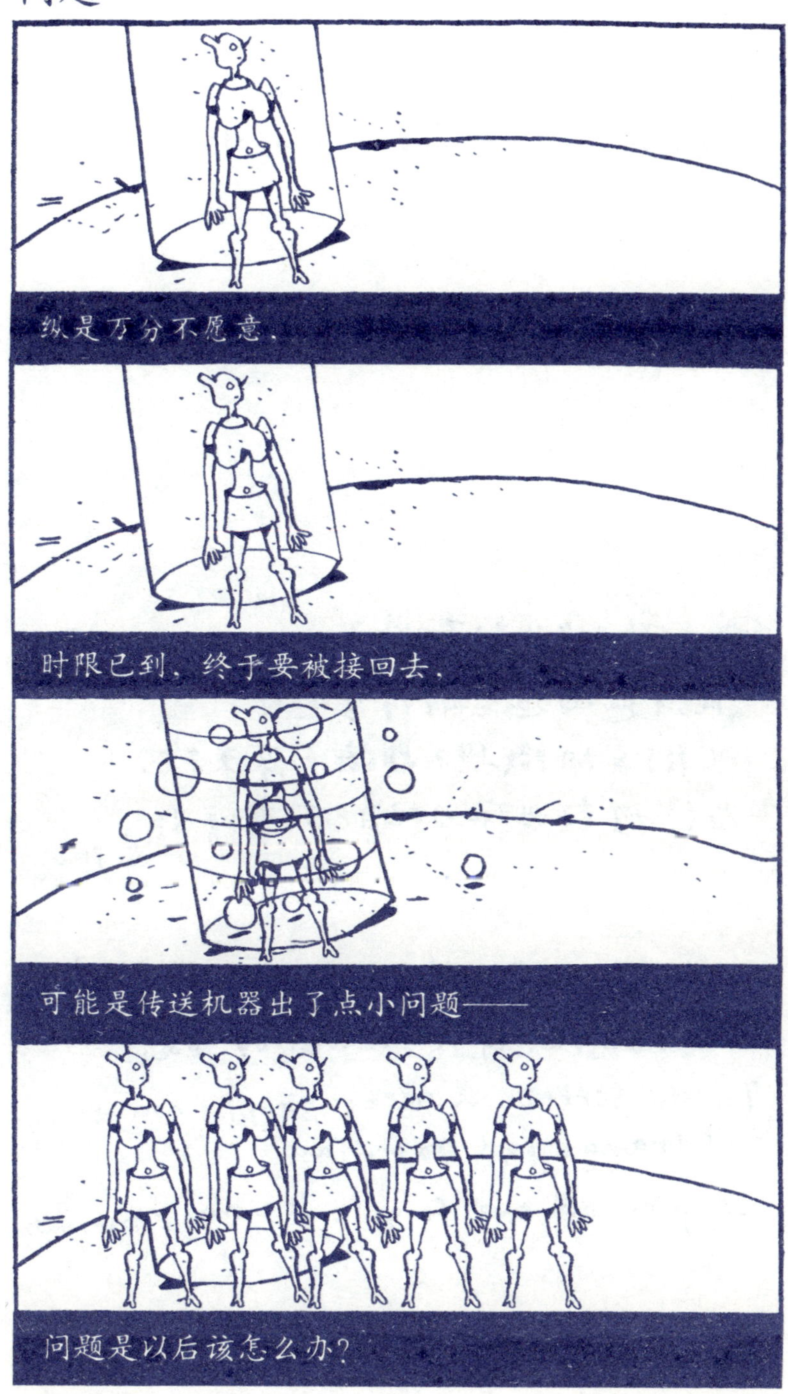

如果在冬夜一件行李

If On A winter's Night a Suitcase

要到的地方也都到過了，
飄洋過海還是隨時會嘔吐，
大街上相識與不相識的來來去去，
年紀大了記性不好把自己的密碼給忘掉了。

It has been to all the places it wants to visit.
It is nauseating to travel by sea.
In the street, it meets people and things strange and familiar.
It gets old and forgets its own combination.

如果在冬夜一件行李

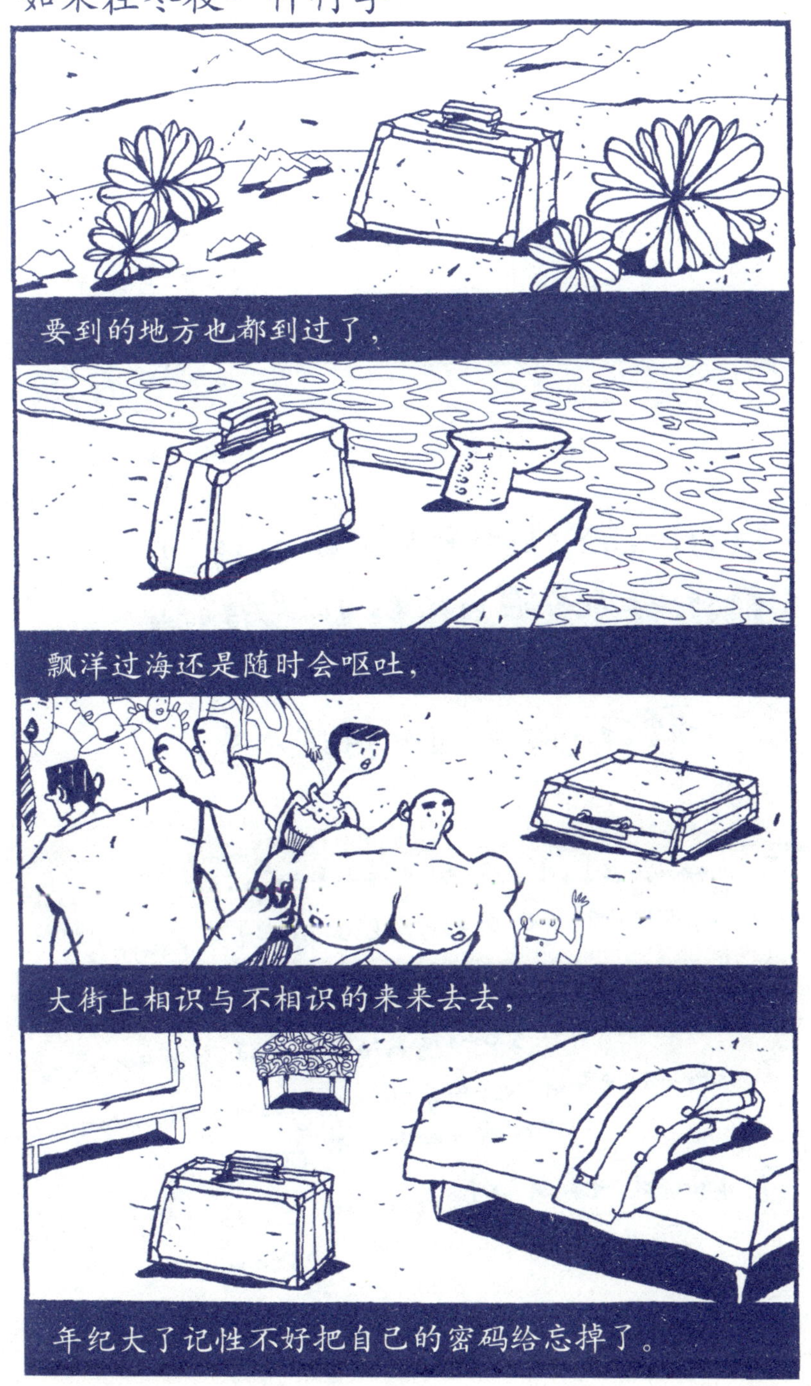
要到的地方也都到过了，
飘洋过海还是随时会呕吐，
大街上相识与不相识的来来去去，
年纪大了记性不好把自己的密码给忘掉了。

家事
Housework.

聽說一切不愉快的都可以洗得一乾乾淨淨。
聽說一切崎嶇曲折都可以熨得貼服，
聽說一切美好的都可以保存新鮮，
聽說一切都可以迅速成事。

I heard that all the unhappiness
could be washed away thoroughly.
I heard that all the problems and roughness
could be straightened out by an iron.
I heard that everything good and wonderful
could be kept fresh.
I heard that everything could be finished
in an instance.

家事

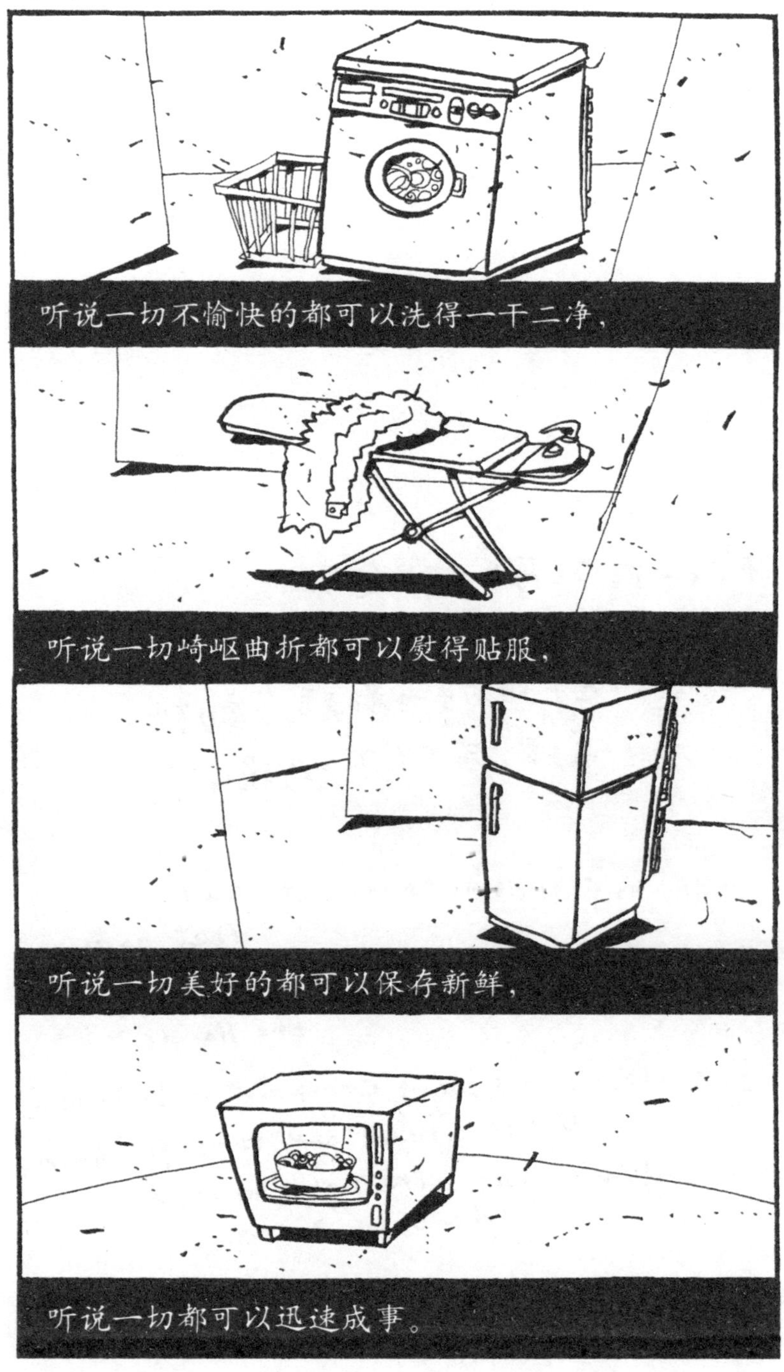
听说一切不愉快的都可以洗得一干二净，
听说一切崎岖曲折都可以熨得贴服，
听说一切美好的都可以保存新鲜，
听说一切都可以迅速成事。

手
Hands

摔了一跤就再也站不起來
然後意外的重新發現手的作用。
想不到左手跟右手也都競爭劇烈，
為爭一長短，右手先下手為强。

After he fell down he can not stand up on his feet again

Unexpectedly he discovers the new use of the hands.

but there is a severe competition between the left hand and the right hand.

In order to win, the right hand does whatever it can.

手

摔了一跤就再也站不起来，
然后意外的重新发现手的作用，
想不到左手跟右手也都竞争剧烈，
为争一长短，右手先下手为强。

禮
Gift

送花給她怕花會凋謝.
送糖給她怕她吃了會太胖.
送錢給她未免太直接.
就送她一個吻。

I'm afraid the flowers may die if I send her flowers.

I'm afraid she might gain weight if I send her candies.

I'm afraid it would be too forward if I send her money.

It would be best to send her a kiss

礼

雜耍
Vaudeville

相識非偶然，
果然一發不可收拾，
因為他可笑所以大家都可以笑。
少許錯誤是可以原諒的。

The meeting is predestined.
There's no end to it once it gets started.
Everybody laughs because he is so funny
Nobody would mind about such minor mistakes

杂耍

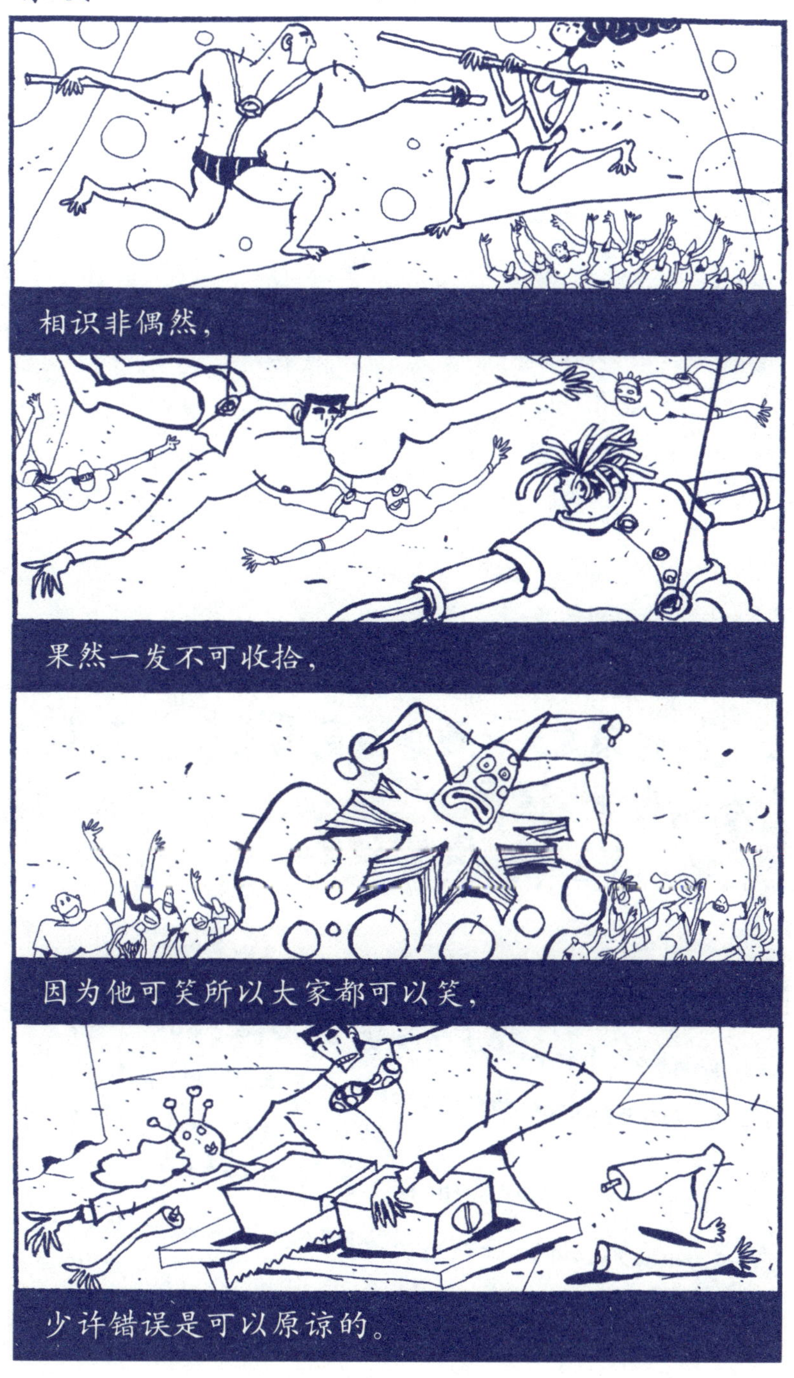

魔術
Magic

搖身一變他就變了個魔術師.
一天到晚變走美女變出白兔變着變着都亂了.
餓了變出一張床.
累了變出一桌豐盛的菜.

He turns into a magician all of a sudden
He makes beautiful girls and rabbits appear
and disappear from morning till night.
He gets confused.

A bed appears when he is hungry.
A sumptuous meal appears when he is tired.

魔术

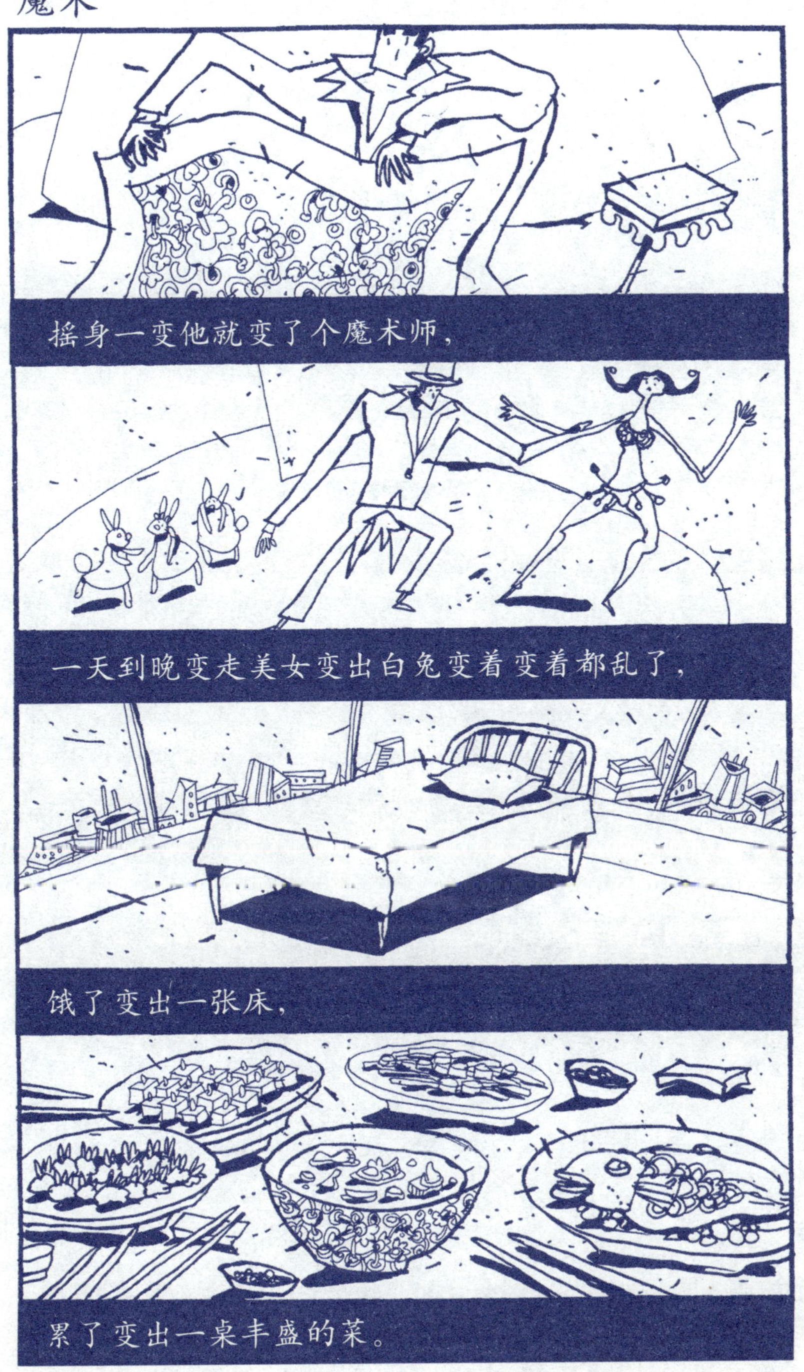

我的天的创作思维和形式手法进入了一个稳实的模式，
心思开始转换到其他的漫画题材和格式上，
当中有几乎同步的《三七廿一》短篇漫画故事的结集，
有《我的天》的兄弟姊妹篇《小明》，《我的天使》和
《少年得志》有一次性的《废画》，
发展下来更有以关系以性别议题为内容的《爱到死》，
角色造型和叙事方法都采取了更面向大众的尝试。
先后推出《爱到死》五本结集，
亦有短期专栏《GoGo & GoGo》。
除了个人创作，也策划了四期独立漫画杂志《Cockroach》，
以不定期不固定题材的方法征集港台以至内地的各自精彩
的漫画家的作品，亦在平面出版以外，
轻度开发产品和组织本地和海外的展览。

看来最蓬勃热闹之际，竟又是预告了冷静期的开始。

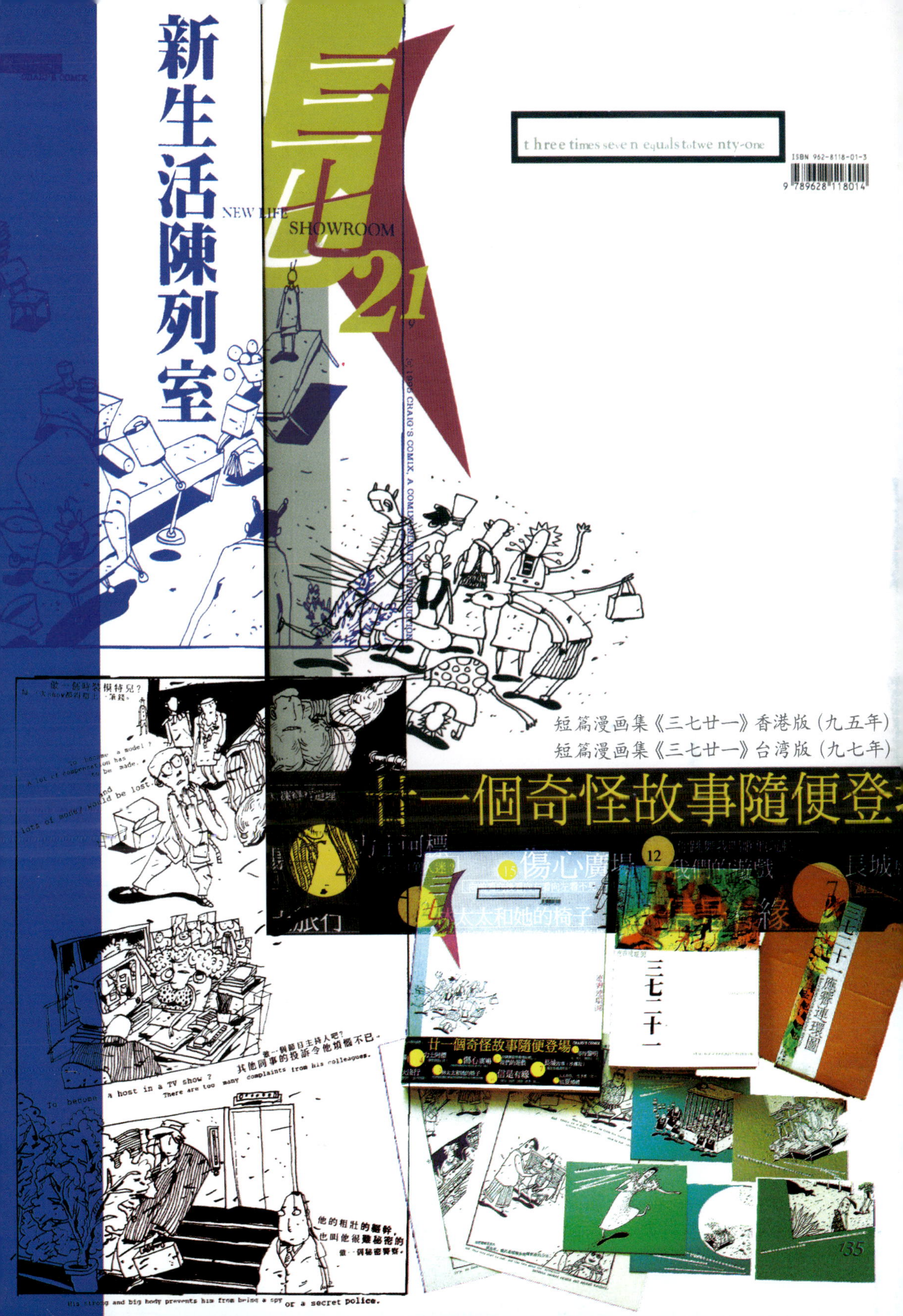

短篇漫画集《三七廿一》香港版(九五年)
短篇漫画集《三七廿一》台湾版(九七年)

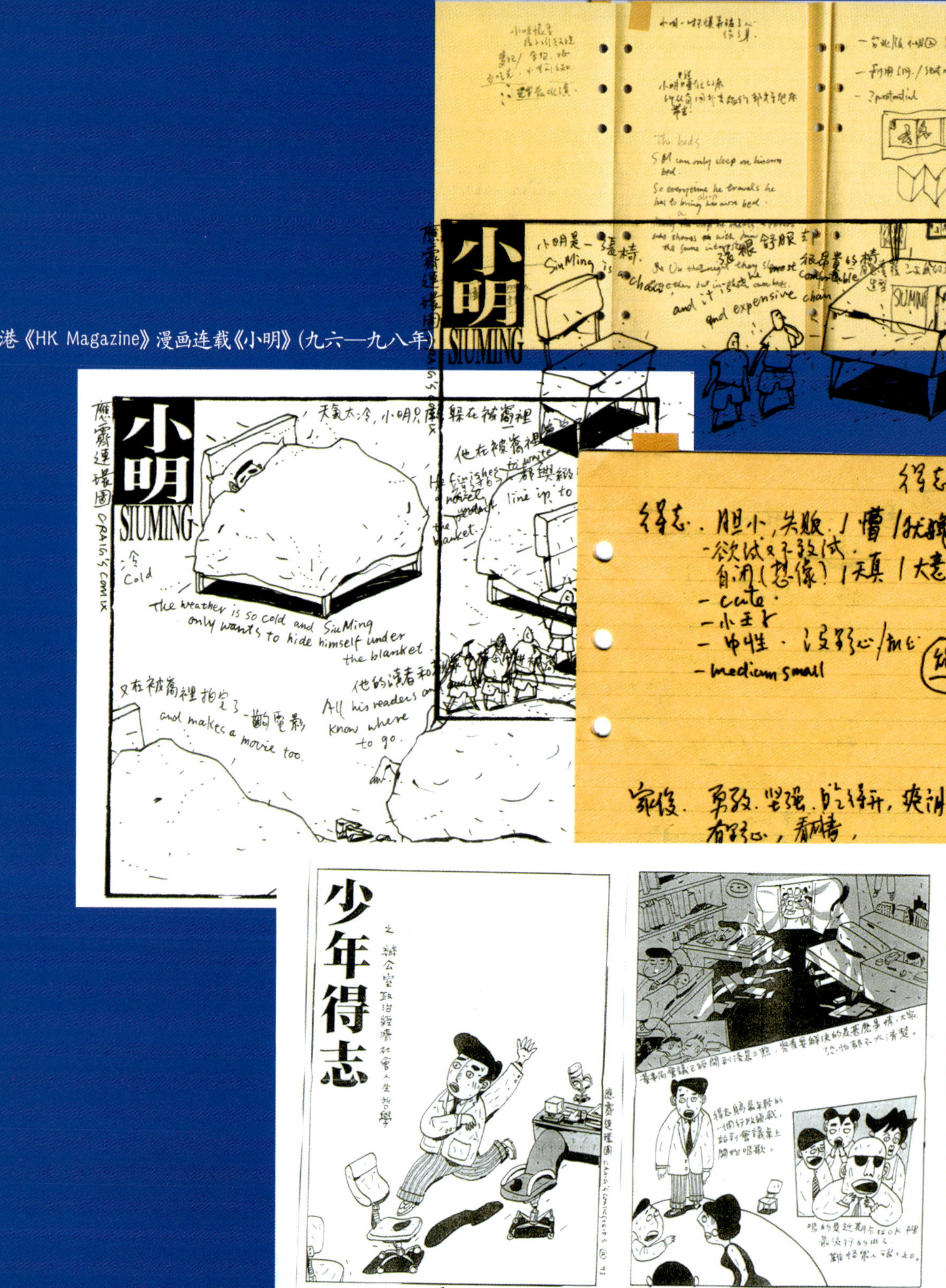

香港《HK Magazine》漫画连载《小明》(九六—九八年)

漫画专栏《少年得志》(九五—九六年)

漫画《我的天使》（九七年）

漫画卡《想你》

《你是我的我是你的》（九六—九七年）

香港《HK Magazine》漫画连载《Love Kills》（〇〇—〇一年）

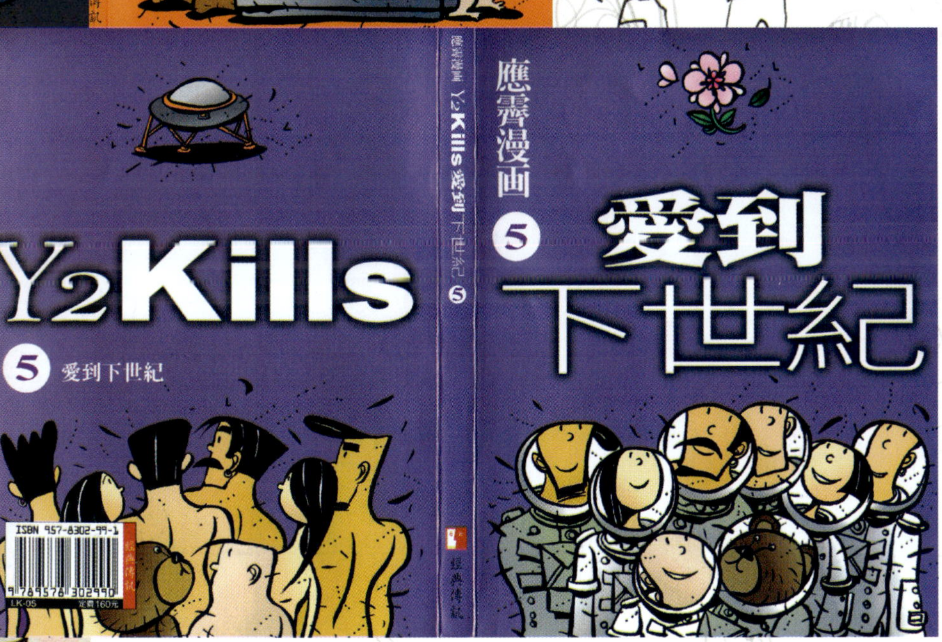

漫画系列《爱到死》一至五册(九九—〇〇年)

《太阳报》漫画专栏《GoGo & GoGo》（九九年）

漫画集《废画》（九六年）

Aids Concern 艾滋关怀漫画集《一场安全性游戏》（九七年）

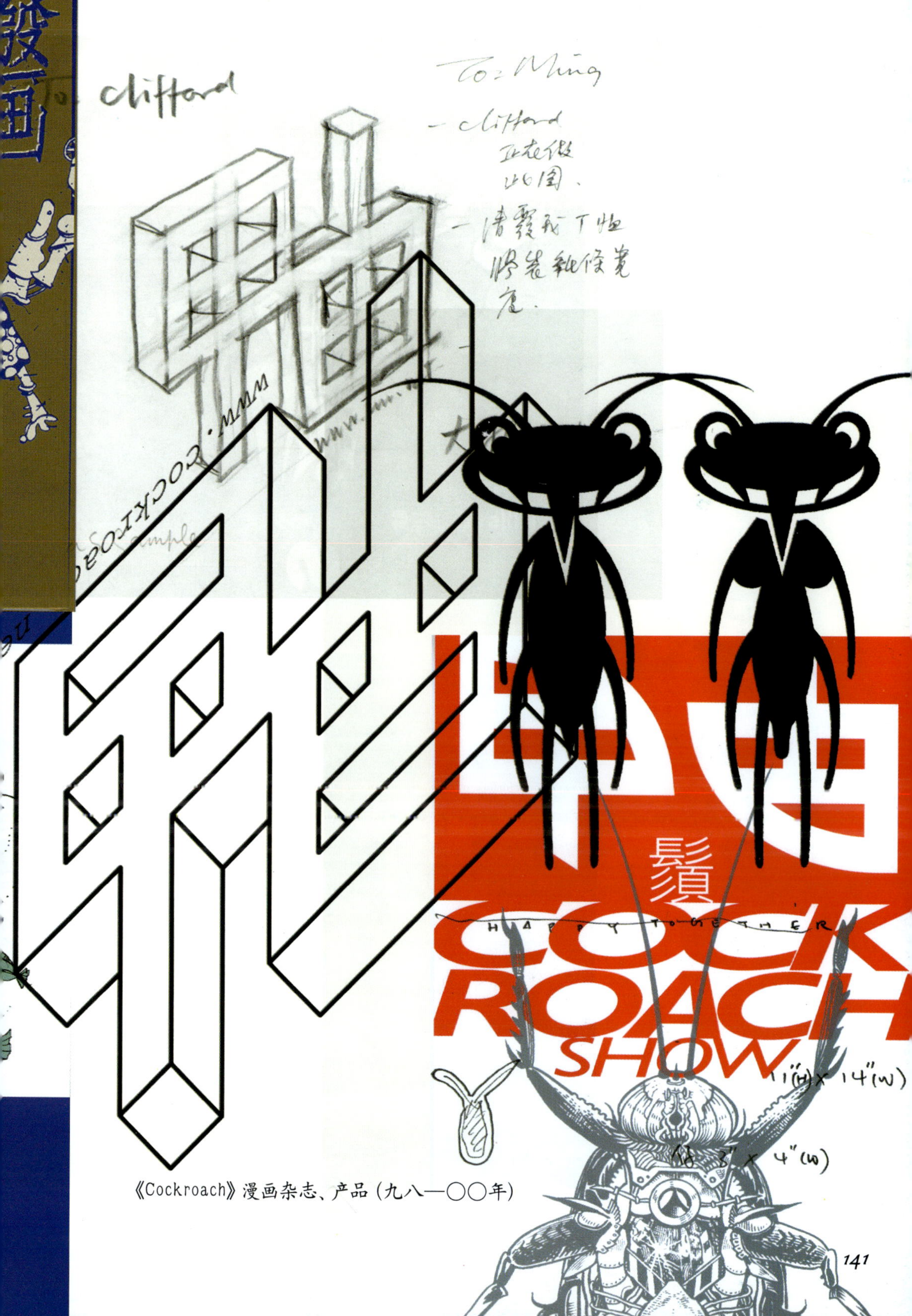

《Cockroach》漫画杂志、产品（九八—〇〇年）

COCKROACH
00春季号
spring issue
99春季號
spring issue
98冬季号
winter issue
創刊號
傑少

欧阳应霁的连环漫画图《三七廿一》、《我地》等系列令人印象深刻，
人物、空间（显见香港景观特点）、单格、线条在涂鸦里张狂流动，
宽臀扁胸的男女、植物、外星人……
伴着黑点点随意摆放，文字（或无）不仅是对话框，也是个人的符号书写，
他说："《我的天》那一时期的作品们，倾向前卫、实验，
到后来《爱到死》系列生活化的态度，不过是形式上的变化，
作品仍旧也一定偷渡些怪里怪气的想法。
经营漫画一段很长的日子，以前漫画承载许多政治意识左右派的宣传，
当社会潮流不再如此专断，为什么不改变一下，把严肃转化通俗，
我愈发觉得一个媒体应该弹性地和更多人沟通而非逞个人表现，
所以各种宽度都去摸索，试图与一般人在一起。"
《幼儿动物园》、《同性四分亲》里，反而是左右简白对照的阅读动线，
文本变得口语，有何不可？

在欧阳应霁可见的作品里，多少会准确—不准确提点到的，
主要是性别和空间这两个议题，飘忽、按捺着哲学氛围，
他则回应："有人看不懂那些关于社会、地域的逻辑，
但那完全是不小心练习出来的气氛。
别人捡拾片段，我只是想到如何诱发观者的开放性，
以性别说来，因为我觉得'作为一个人'应该找寻个体定位，
男女无所别，可说是一种'有没有能力决定人生'积极的态度。
人会变的，将刻板的要求与标准，一一打破，
选择无性／同性／异性，对应到某一时期最对的状态，
我意图和'自己准备要变的人'说话！"
不说大道理，漫画用以凝聚同志并不孤单的共识。

—— 林倩如　〇二年十二月

沉思者

thinker

活在這個年頭要做一個沉思者確實不容易，
要思想的都思想過了沒有甚麼可以繼續思想，
同樣的姿勢坐得太久肌肉都酸痛不堪，
而且暴露太多沒有新鮮感也再引不起觀眾興趣。

It is not easy to be a thinker at such a time.
He has thought of everything, and there's nothing left to think anymore.
His body aches for remaining in the same position for too long.
And he has exposed so much of his body for so long that people start losing interest.

沉思者

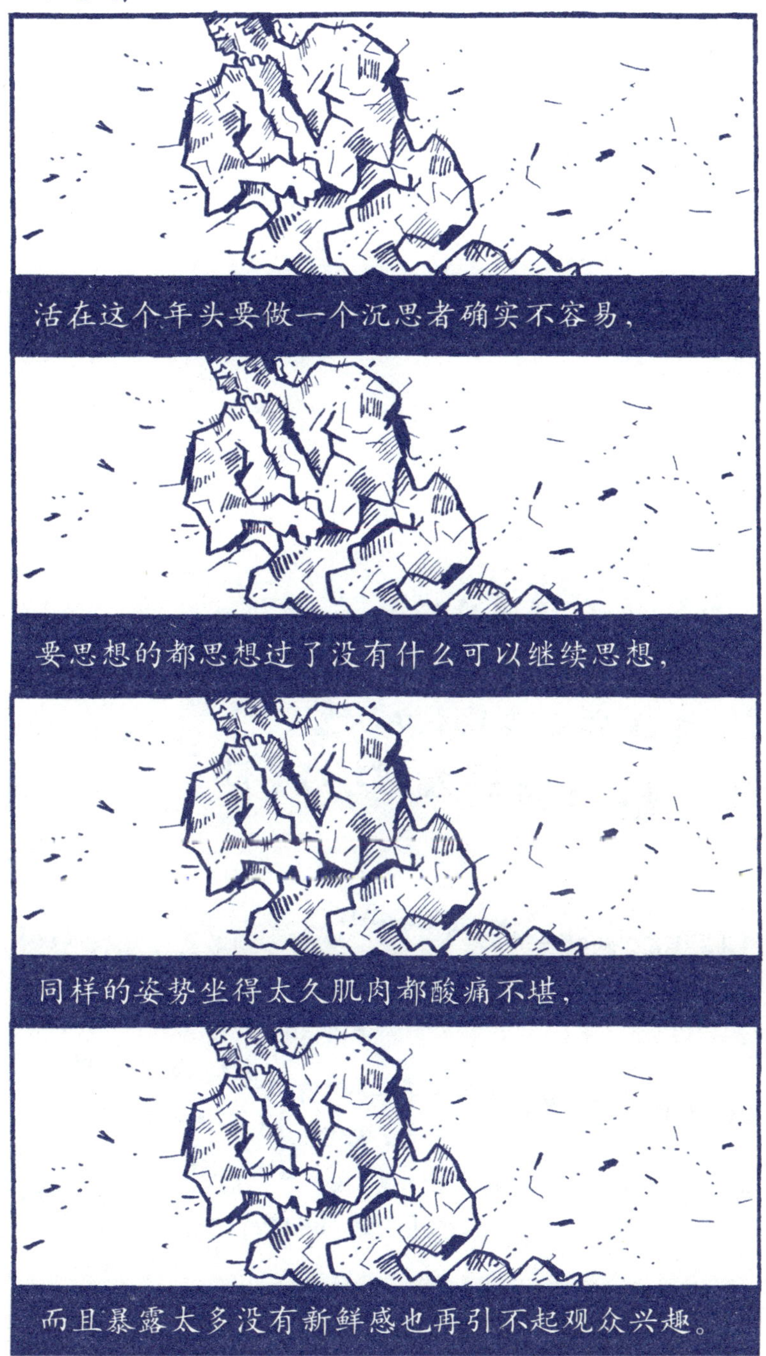
活在这个年头要做一个沉思者确实不容易，
要思想的都思想过了没有什么可以继续思想，
同样的姿势坐得太久肌肉都酸痛不堪，
而且暴露太多没有新鲜感也再引不起观众兴趣。

飛人

Flying Man

事到如今算是成功了
可是離了地又始終覺得不踏實.
事態發展往往不如人意.
飛人生活得花一點時間去適應.

He has made it after all.
But he doesn't feel right to have his feet
off the ground.
It is not very satisfactory as how things
are developing.
It'll take some time to adjust
himself to being a flying man.

飞人

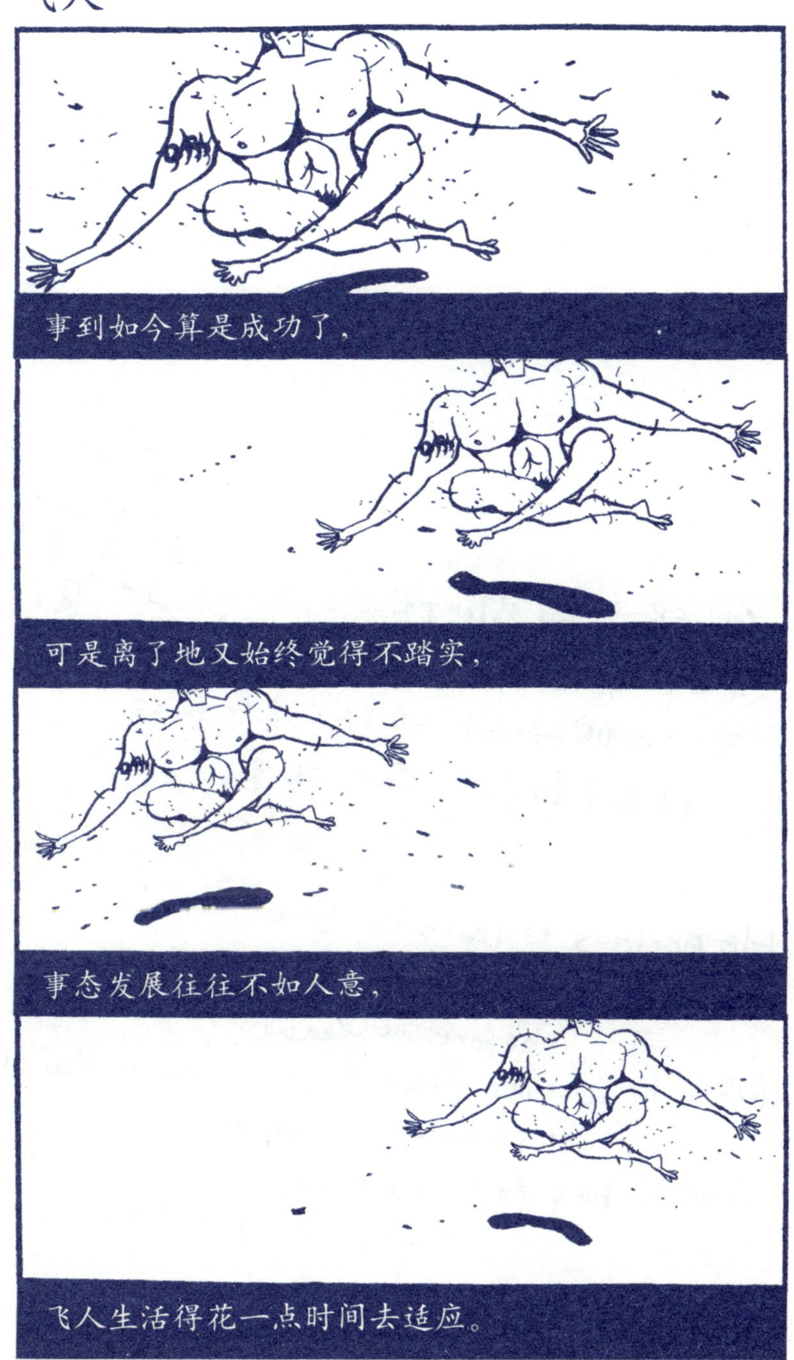

記掛

Cares

他決定要離開地球，
走之前痛痛快快的吃了一頓日本魚生。
到了那個不知名的小星球他突然記起，
他忘了對最新一期的彩票。

He decides to leave the Earth
He has a very sumptuous Sashimi meal
before he leaves.
When he reaches that little unknown planet
he suddenly remembers…
That he has forgotten to check
his lottery ticket.

记挂

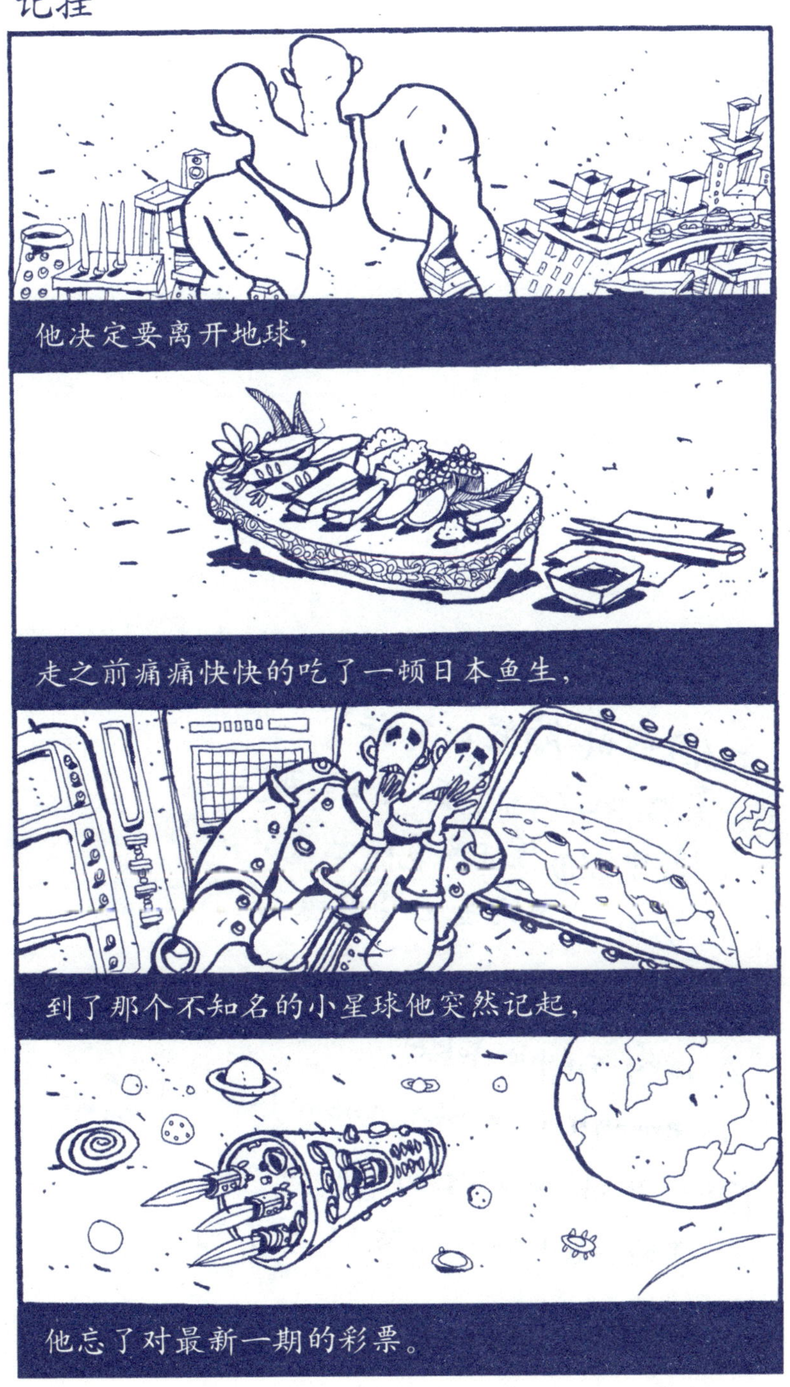
他决定要离开地球，
走之前痛痛快快的吃了一顿日本鱼生，
到了那个不知名的小星球他突然记起，
他忘了对最新一期的彩票。

哭笑之間

Between Laughing and Crying

一個如此簡單的笑話，
竟然把他們都笑得瘋了。
當中一個笑下去竟然死了。
另外一個於是大哭起來。

A very simple joke
Is enough to make them laugh like crazy
One of them dies of laughing,
The other one starts crying.

哭笑之间

過日子

Pastime

到林中去思想，
到海邊去歡樂，
到原野去漫步，
到公司去上班。

Go to the woods to think.
Go to the beach to have some fun
Go to wander in the wilderness
Go to the office to work.

过日子

路

Road

請用十五分鐘將一段可以用十五分鐘走完的路

好好走一次。

或者改用三十分鐘把路慢慢走。

當然他習慣只用二分鐘一往無前，

沿途還要聽三通電話 其實是頗尷尬的事。

Please spend 15 minutes to walk a road
that would take 15 minutes to finish.

Or spend 30 minutes walking the same
road slowly.

Of course, he is used to finishing the same
distance in 2 minutes

And listening to 3 phone calls at the same
time.

How embarrassing!

路

请用十五分钟将一段可以用十五分钟走完的路好好走一次，
或者改用三十分钟把路慢慢走。
当然他习惯只用二分钟一往无前，
沿途还要听三通电话其实是颇尴尬的事。

别人

Someone Else

早上起来又穿上了别人的鞋，
总是打上了别人的领带就上班了。
办公室里总是接了别人要接的电话，
下班后拿了别人的钥匙回到别人的家。

Get up in the morning and put on someone else's shoes.
Always wear someone else's tie to work.
Always answer someone else's telephone calls in the office.
Take someone else's keys after work and go to someone else's home

别人

早上起来又穿上了别人的鞋，
总是打上了别人的领带就上班了，
办公室里总是接了别人要接的电话，
下班后拿了别人的锁钥回到别人的家。

大掃除

Clean up.

掃最後一粒塵掃走的時候他有點捨不得。
偌大的家裡空空的甚麼也沒有。
每年到了這個時候其實他總想結識新朋友。
可是為了省得掃除，還是自己一個人好。

He finds it very difficult to accept that
he is cleaning up the last piece of dirt.
The big house seems so empty.
He always wants to meet some new friends
this time every year
But when he thinks of the cleaning up he has
to do, He gives up the idea and would
rather be alone.

大扫除

将最后一粒尘扫走的时候他有点舍不得，
偌大的家里空空的什么也没有，
每年到了这个时候其实他总想结识新朋友，
可是为了省得扫除，还是自己一个人好。

後事

Afterwards

散了場故事才開始
下了車才發覺未到站。
花謝了卻是久久的不結果。
上了床熄了燈才知道身邊沒有人。

The story begins only after the show.

Come to realize this is not the right stop
only when the bus is gone.

The fruits will not come out long after
the flowers have fallen.

Come to realize there is no one lying next
to you only after you have turned off the lights
and climbed into bed.

后事

罪

Sin

他走進河裡希望把罪惡洗去
怎知道河水污染得厲害，
不到三分鐘他竟然變了一頭怪獸。
急急上了彼岸他得重新申請做人

He wishes to cleanse his sins in the river.
But the water in the river is so polluted
That he turns into a monster within 3 minutes.
Climbs on the opposite shore and starts a
new life.

罪

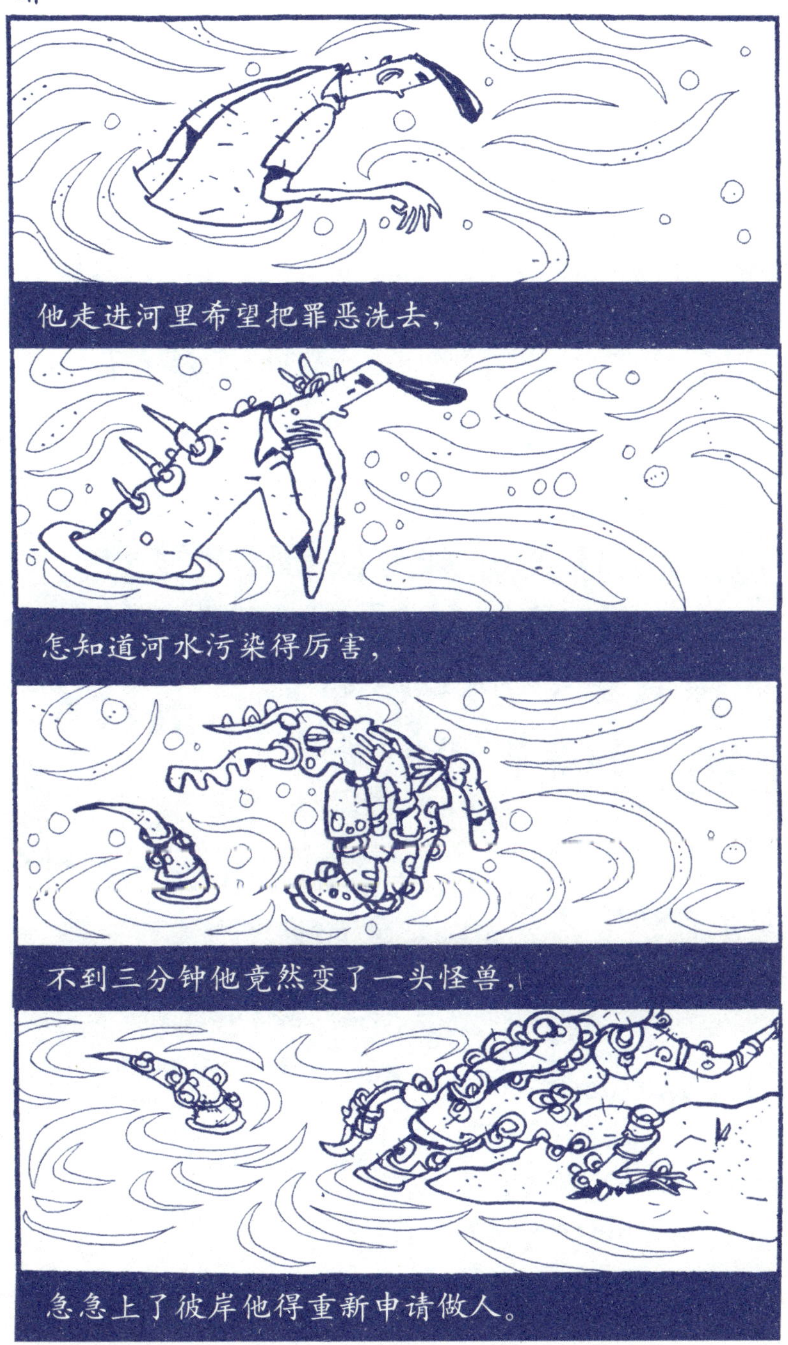
他走进河里希望把罪恶洗去，
怎知道河水污染得厉害，
不到三分钟他竟然变了一头怪兽，
急急上了彼岸他得重新申请做人。

做人難

It's a Difficult Life

牠現在的情況明顯的比想像中複雜
身為禽獸，要超越自己其實有很多方法，
選擇變做人實在並不明智。
茫茫人海中常常要把尾巴藏起來的確不容易。

Its present situation is much more complicated than it appears.

Being an animal, there are numerous ways of surpassing oneself.

It is not very wise indeed to choose to become a man.

It is really very difficult to hide one's tail among thousands of people.

做人难

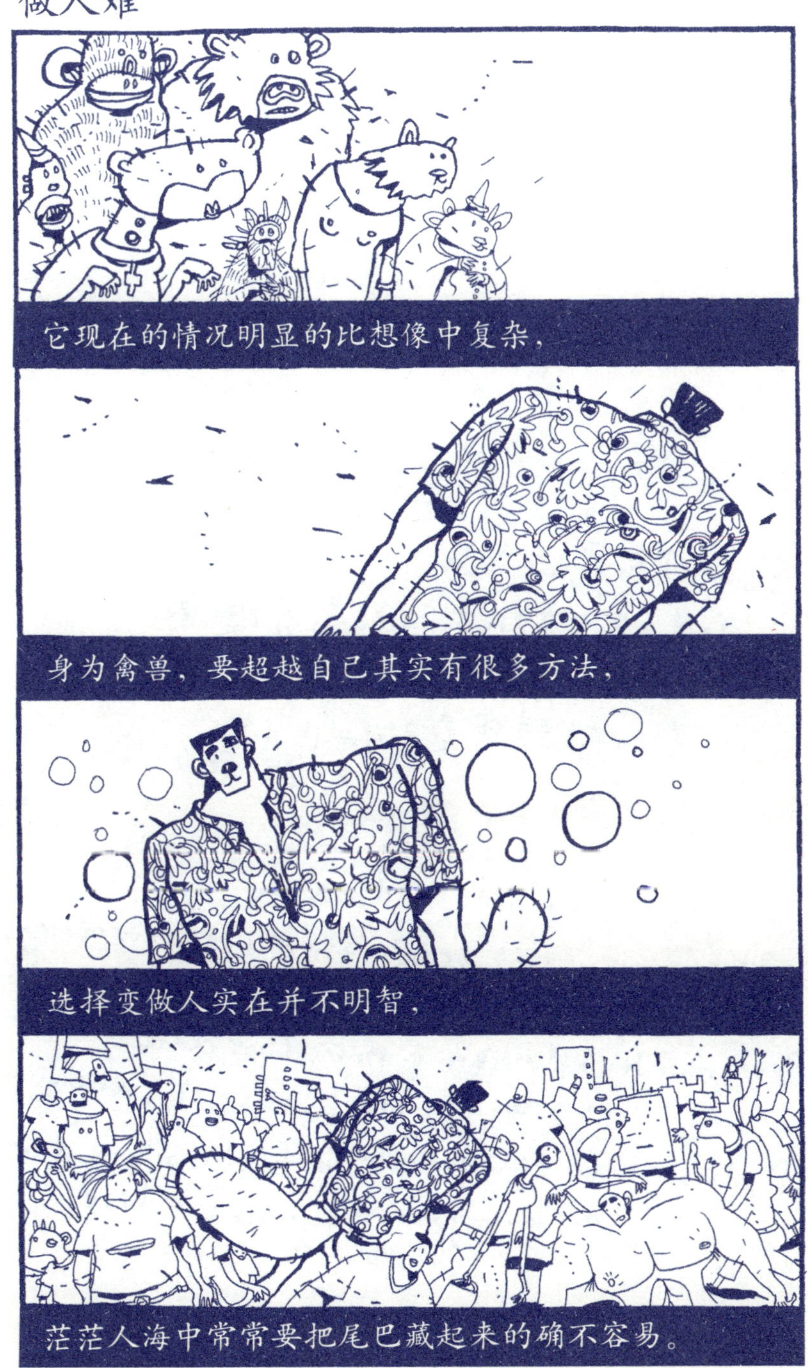
它现在的情况明显的比想像中复杂，
身为禽兽，要超越自己其实有很多方法，
选择变做人实在并不明智，
茫茫人海中常常要把尾巴藏起来的确不容易。

活著

To Live

活到今天實在不容易
可惜大家只對化石和乾屍有興趣
或者可以考慮跳跳原始舞引起大眾注意，
又恐怕被誤會是不可一世的所謂藝術家。

It's not easy to live till now.
It's a pity that people are only interested in fossils and mummies.
He thinks of doing a primitive dance in order to attract people's attention
But is afraid that people might take him for an arrogant so-called artist.

活着

活到今天实在不容易，
可惜大家只对化石和干尸有兴趣，
或者可以考虑跳跳原始舞引起大众注意，
又恐怕被误会是不可一世的所谓艺术家。

晚間新聞

Evening News

是時候看七點半晚間新聞了。
不知道今天晚上是誰報告新聞？
不知道今天晚上的新聞是否夠精彩夠份量。
還是拿上星期五錄影了的晚間新聞出來，比較耐看。

It's time to watch the 7 o'clock news.
So, who is announcing the news tonight?
Wonder if the news tonight would be spectacular and heavy enough.
It'd be better to watch the news taped last Friday. It's more interesting.

晚间新闻

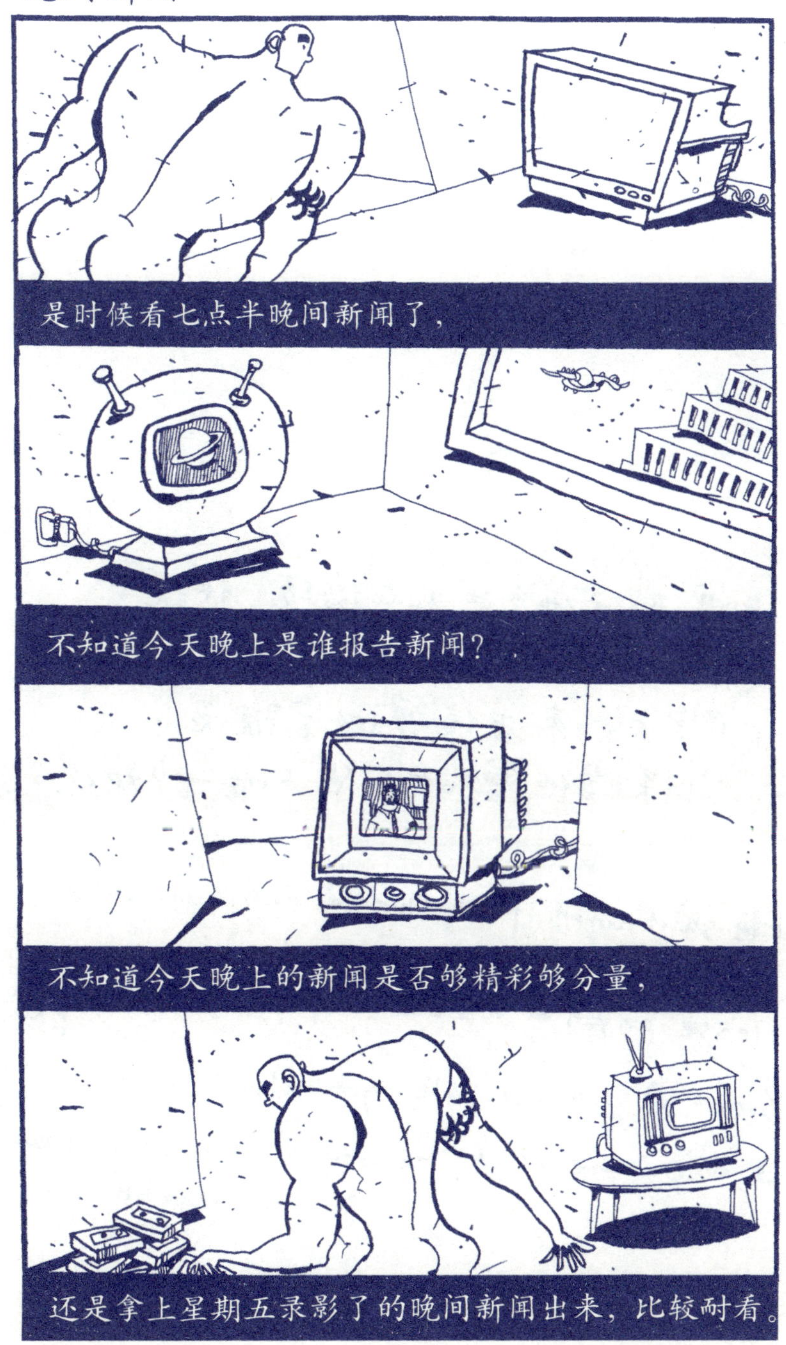
是时候看七点半晚间新闻了，
不知道今天晚上是谁报告新闻？
不知道今天晚上的新闻是否够精彩够分量，
还是拿上星期五录影了的晚间新闻出来，比较耐看。

遺痕

Leaving Marks

如果有一天他突然死在街頭，他說。
請替他準備一罐A字牌白色漆油。
A字牌漆油信譽好字號老，
它保證他會在世上留下唯一的痕迹。

He said that if he should die suddenly
in the street one day.
please buy him a bucket of Brand A white paint.
Brand A is a reliable, good old brand,
It'd ensure that he would leave his marks
on earth.

遗痕

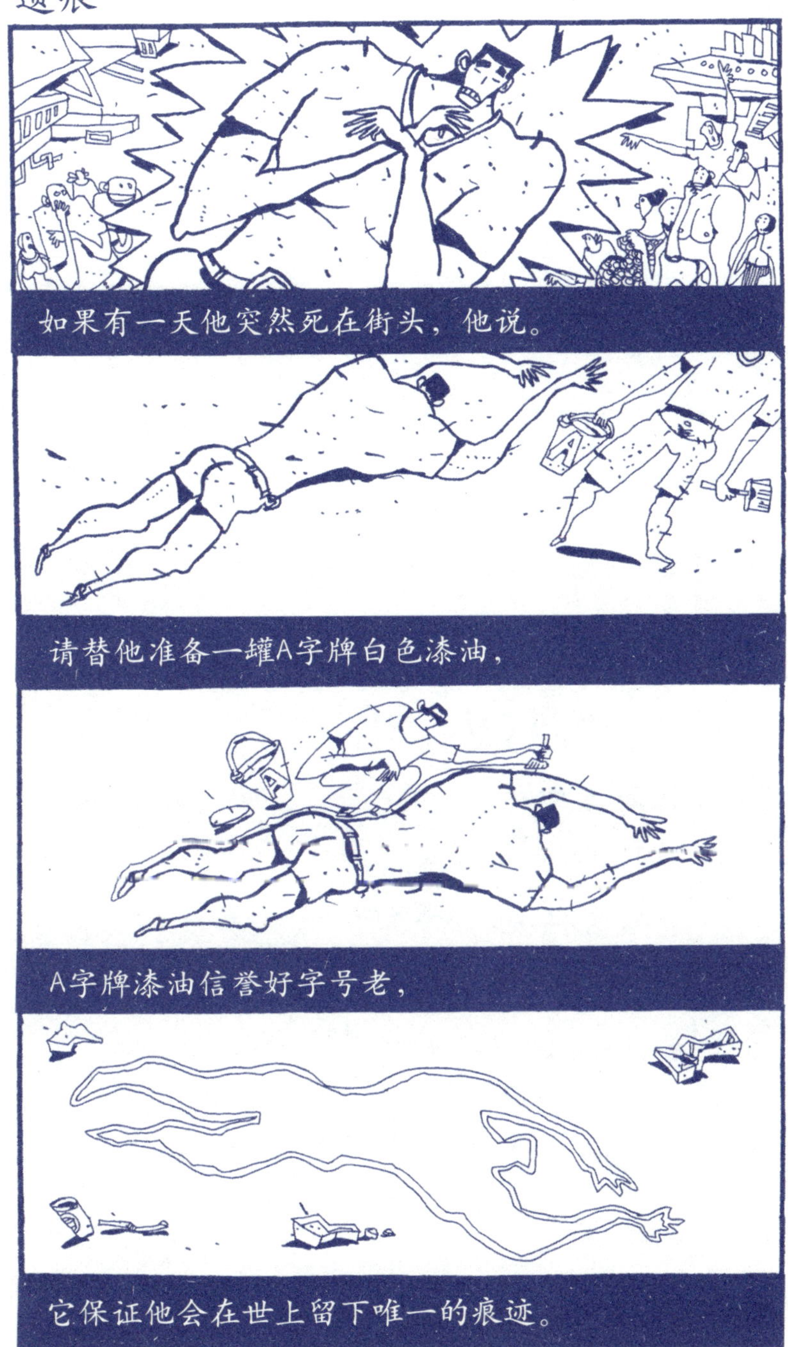
如果有一天他突然死在街头，他说。
请替他准备一罐A字牌白色漆油，
A字牌漆油信誉好字号老，
它保证他会在世上留下唯一的痕迹。

藉口

Cause

他為了遠大理想，
他為了生活，
他為了愛人，
他只是為了興趣。

He does it for an ideal
He does it for a living
He does it for love.
He does it for fun.

借口

新年愿望

New Year's Resolution

希望做一隻思路清晰的獨立的狗。
能够隨時準備迎接大時代的挑戰。
從今開始注重小節如不隨地大小便。
大事方面要能決定應否隨主人移民。

Wish that I could be a sober-minded and independent dog.
In order to take the challenge of the big time.
I'd be careful about minor things from now on.
like not to relieve myself in the public.
And be decisive on major issues like whether to emigrate with my master.

新年愿望

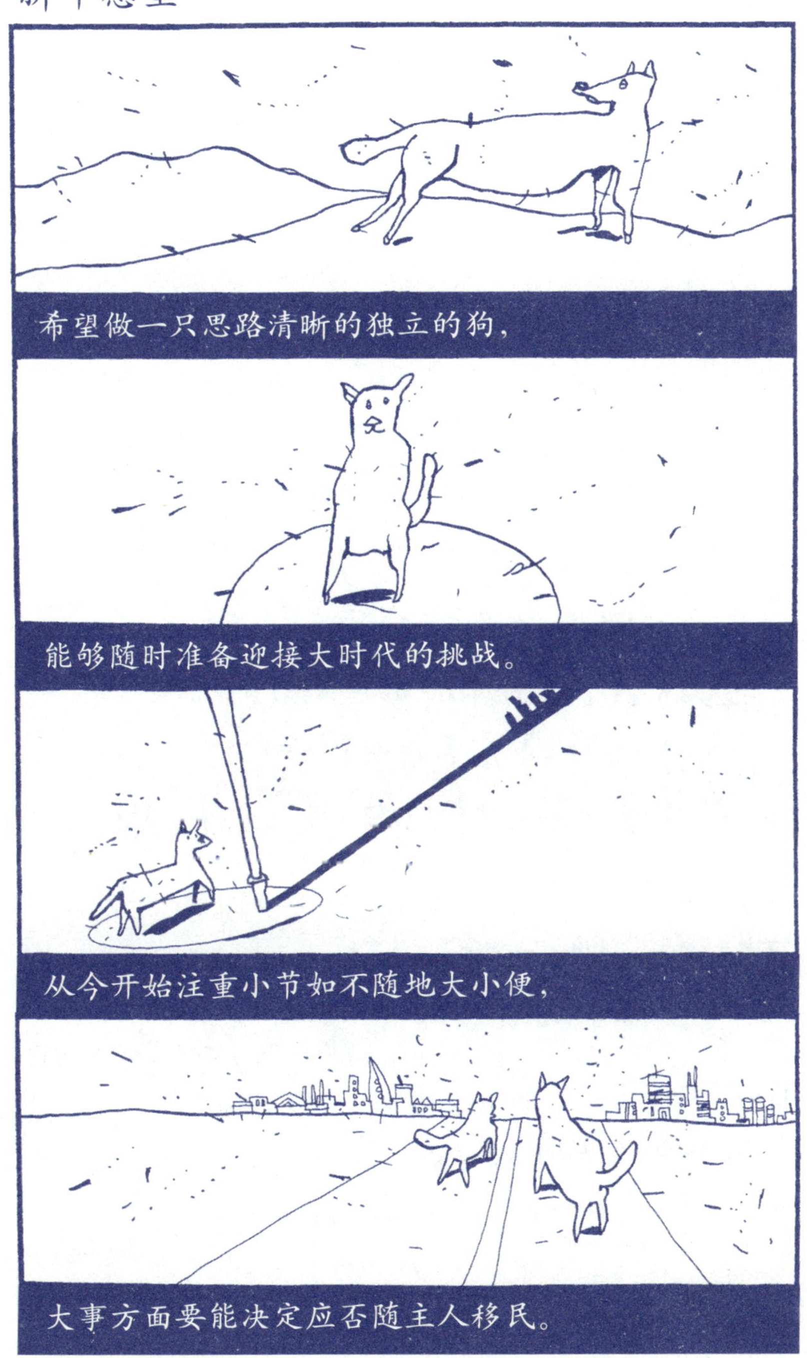
希望做一只思路清晰的独立的狗，
能够随时准备迎接大时代的挑战。
从今开始注重小节如不随地大小便，
大事方面要能决定应否随主人移民。

生趣

The Fun of Life

事到如今實在沒有辦法唯有跳下去，
幾秒鐘之後大概一切也都了結，
可是這次墮落看來永不終止，
在高速中他找到了生之動力，生之樂趣。

There's no way out now, The only way is to jump.
Everything would be fine
after a few seconds.
But the fall seems never to end.
In the speed of falling, he finds
the purpose and the fun of life.

生趣

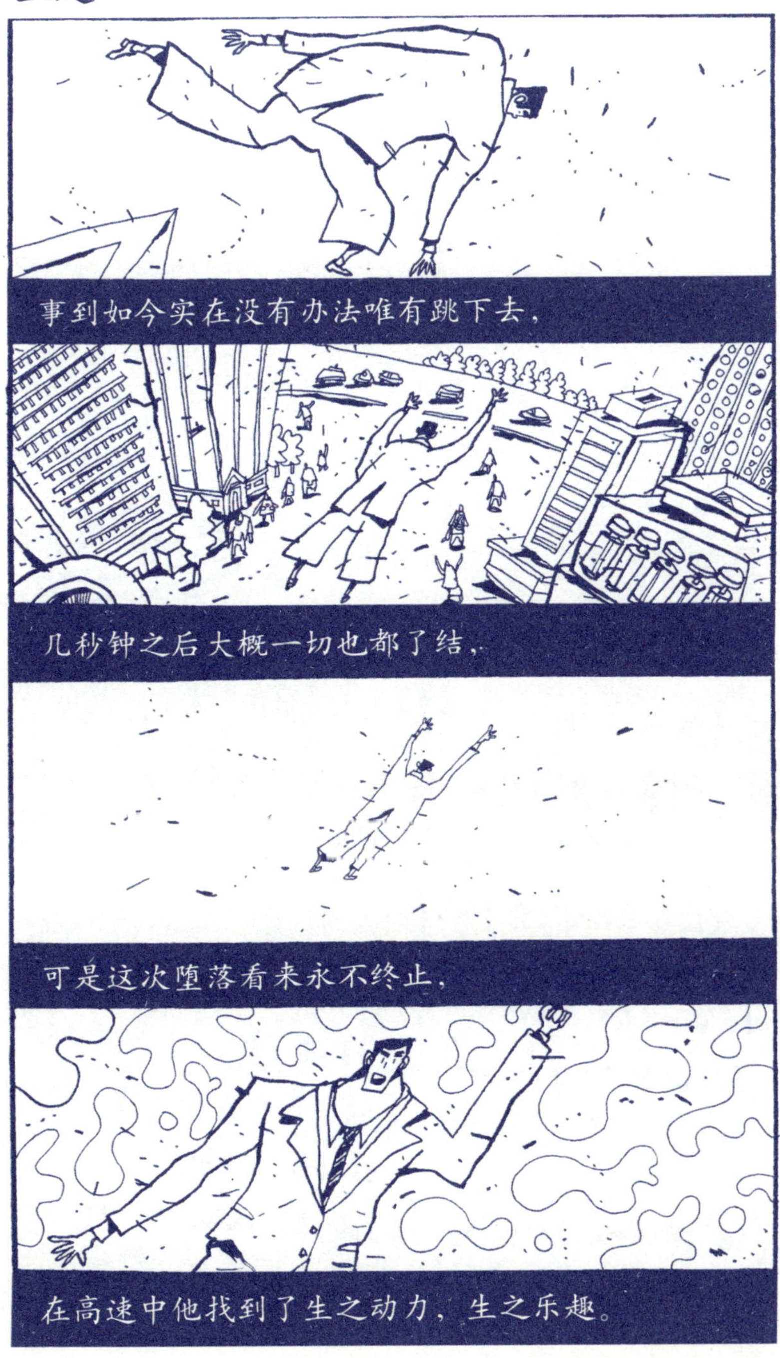
事到如今实在没有办法唯有跳下去，
几秒钟之后大概一切也都了结，
可是这次堕落看来永不终止，
在高速中他找到了生之动力，生之乐趣。

願

Three wishes

在縱身一跳之前他許下三個願望，

願世界和平，

願香港繁榮安定，

願自己永遠快樂。

He makes three wishes before he jumps.

He wishes for world peace.

He wishes for the stability and prosperity of Hong Kong.

He wishes he'd be happy forever.

在纵身一跳之前他许下三个愿望，

愿世界和平，

愿香港繁荣安定，

愿自己永远快乐。

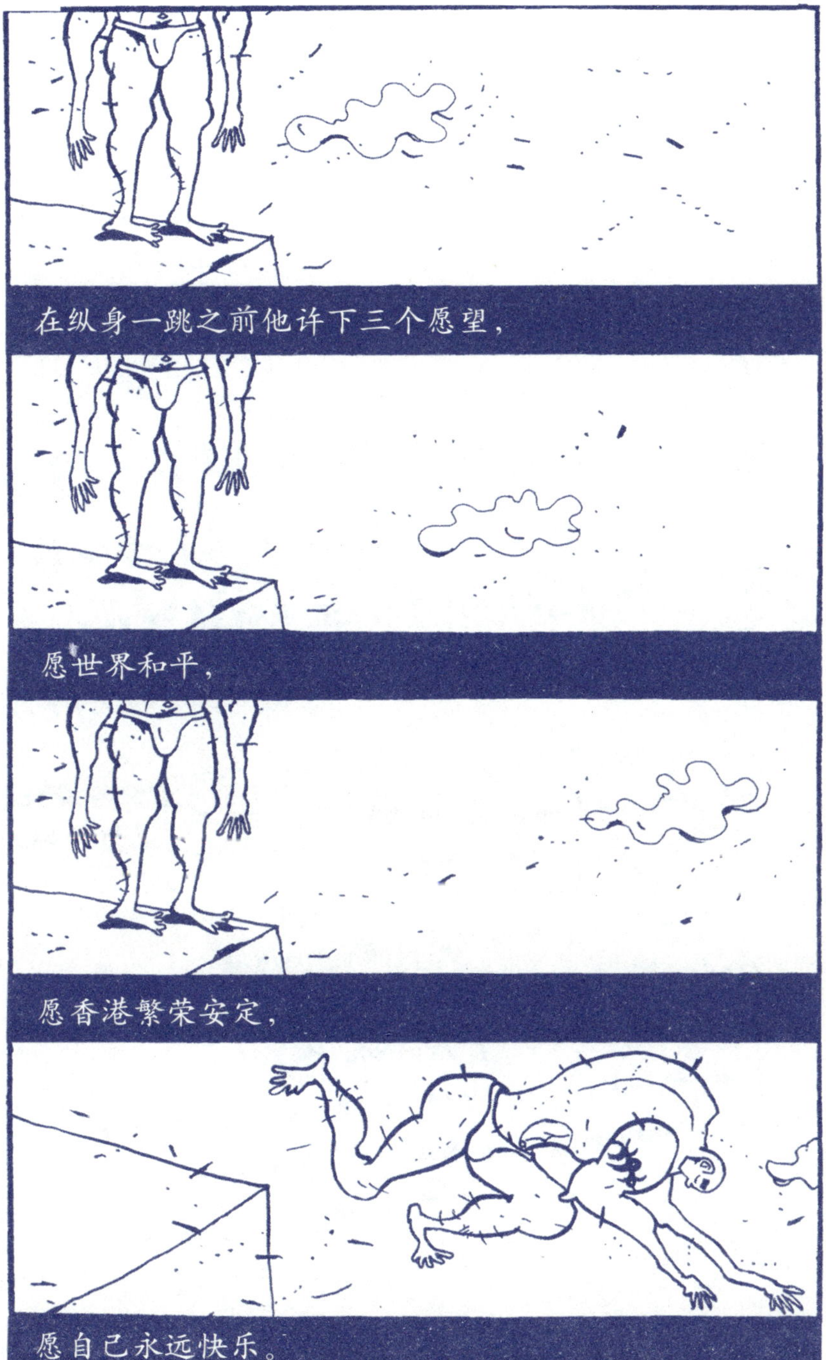

多謝

Thanks.

他在台上再一次多謝第二段第四排穿紅衣的觀眾，
再一次多謝昨晚宵夜的那碗清湯牛腩伊麵。
再一次多謝觀塘偉業街流浪的貓貓狗狗，
再一次多謝夏天的雨秋天的風和冬天的太陽。

Standing on the stage, he thanks once again the one dressed in red in the 2nd seat of the 4th row in the audience.
He says thanks once more to the bowl of beef hoddle after the show last night
And thanks again to the stray cats and dogs in Park Avenue of North Point.
And thanks one more time to the rains in summer, the breeze in autumn and the sun in Winter.

多谢

他在台上再一次多谢第二段第四排穿红衣的观众，
再一次多谢昨晚宵夜的那碗清汤牛腩伊面，
再一次多谢观塘伟业街流浪的猫猫狗狗，
再一次多谢夏天的雨秋天的风和冬天的太阳。

歷史性訪問

A Historic Interview

對於未來的展望她實在有太多看法，
訪問錄影完了她仍然滔滔不絕。
歷史就是如此這般的發展下去……
進入新紀元自有一番新氣象。

She has a lot to say about the future.
She could not stop even after the interview
Thus history progresses,
Entering a new era with new development.

历史性访问

对于未来的展望她实在有太多看法，
访问录影完了她仍然滔滔不绝。
历史就是如此这般的发展下去……
进入新纪元自有一番新气象。

結果

Fruitless

明明是約好了一同化蝶

他卻自作主張變作花，

一怒之下她召來一群蜂，

蜜盡花亡以他不能結果。

They have a pact from the very start
to reincarnate as butterflies.

Somehow, he changes his mind and
becomes a flower.

She turns sour and furious,
and gathers a whole swarm of bees.
The essence of the flower is all drawn and
he can bear no fruits anymore.

结果

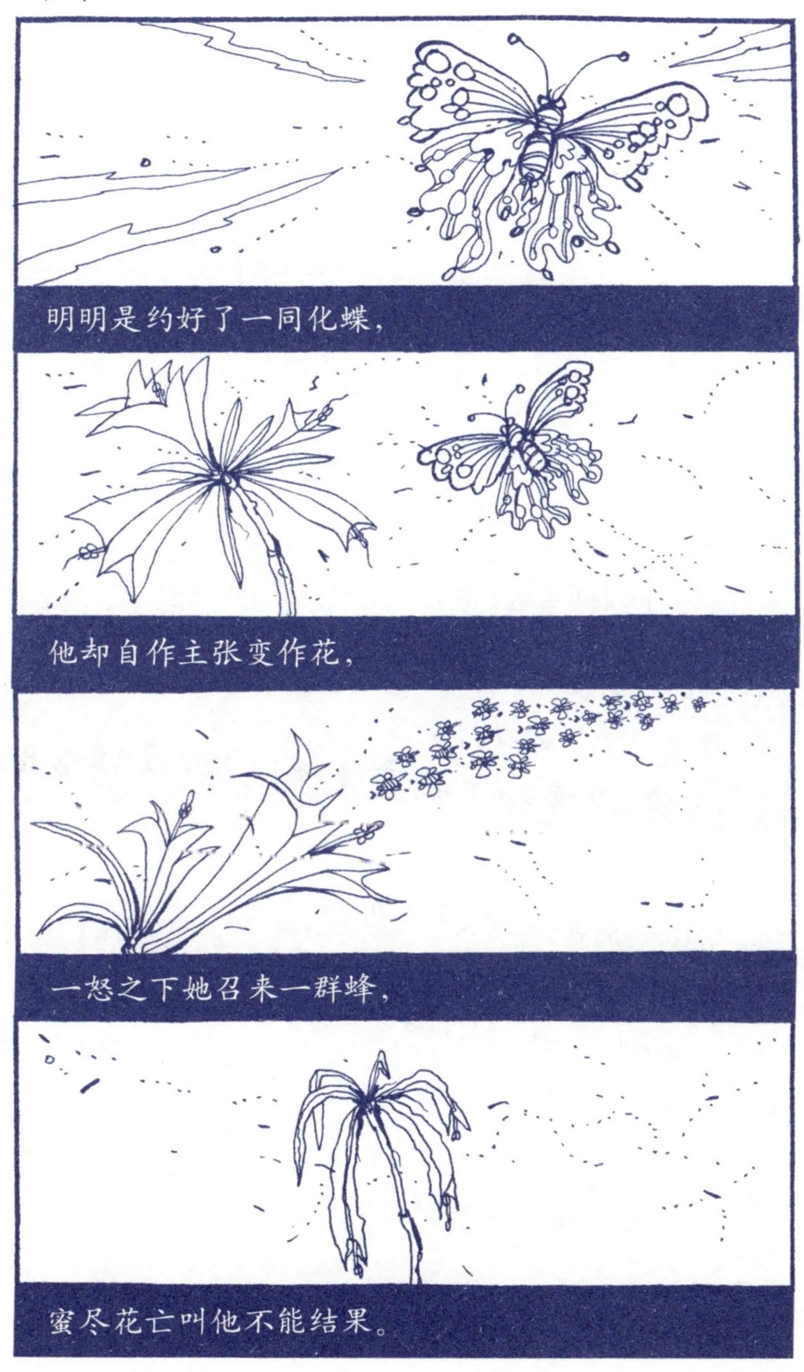

回家
Home sweet Home

回家的感覺真好。
雖然養的三隻貓，兩隻狗和五隻蜥蜴都已餓死。
花還是開得好好的。
電冰箱裡還剩下兩盒美味的微波爐食品。

It's always nice to be home.
Though all my pets, three cats, two dogs
and five lizards are all dead,
The flowers are still blooming beautifully.
And there are still two packs of
microwave food in the freezer.

回家

回家的感觉真好。
虽然养的三只猫，两只狗和五只蜥蜴都已饿死，
花还是开得好好的，
电冰箱里还剩下两盒美味的微波炉食品。

看海的日子

Room with a sea View

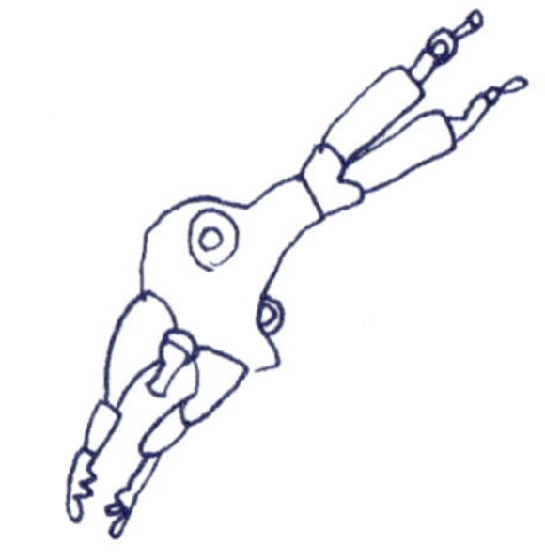

看海，

照樣有游魚，

照樣有各式垃圾，

照樣有逃難或者殉情的將腐未腐的屍骨

Looking out into the Sea.

I see fish swimming around as usual

I see all sorts of rubbish as usual

I see rotting remains of refugees.

and lovers who took their own lives.

看海的日子

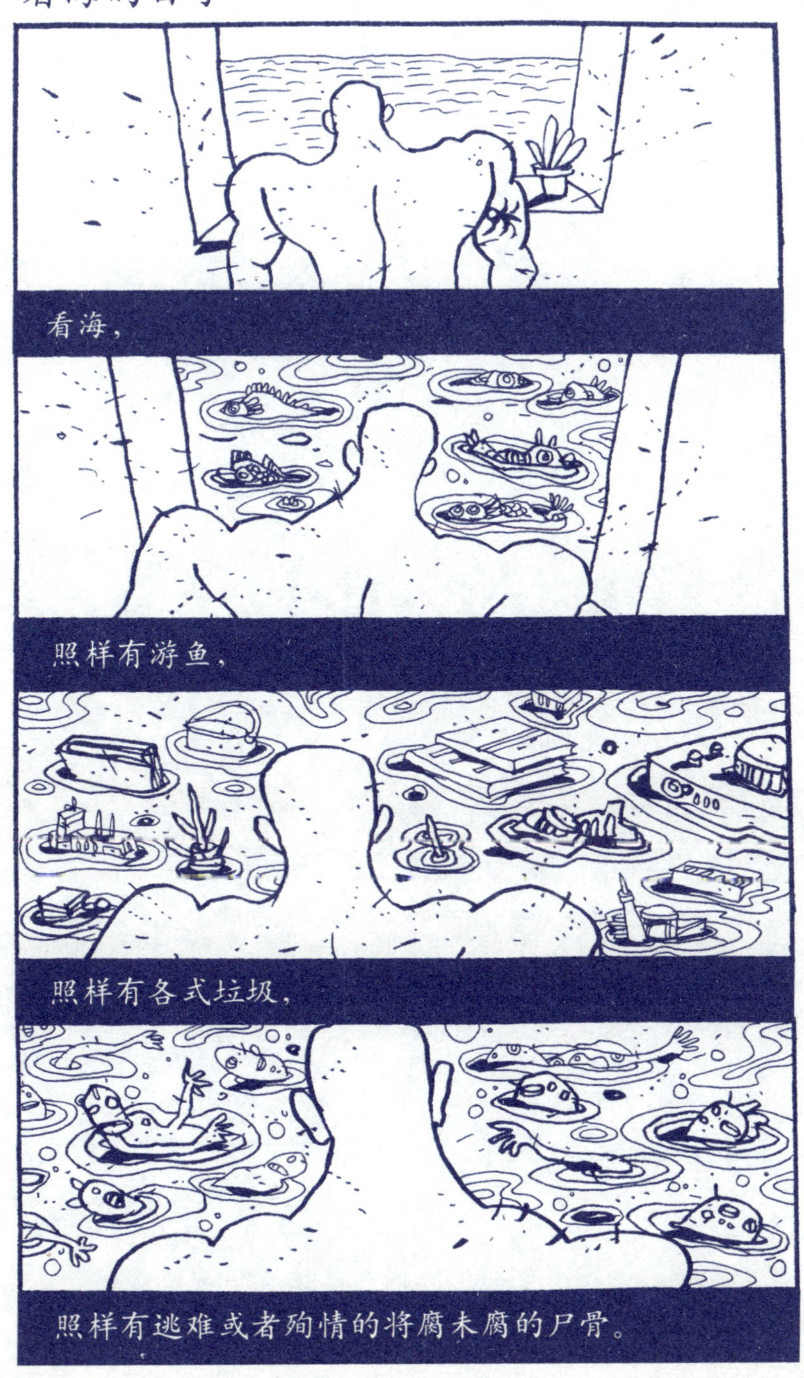

刻意放缓脚步，反思自己跟至爱漫画的真正关系，
如何保持漫画创作原创性和实验性的饱满能量和新鲜力度？
又如何计划和开发漫画作为流行文化商品的可能性？
如何协调如何启动？
看来都需要沉住气仔细考量。

《四九三十六，应霁的四格情事》漫画装置展（〇三年）

《乃霑应霁父子双拼》装置展（〇〇年）

台北《饮食》杂志《食色》漫画专栏（〇五年）

香港《明报周刊》《我的天》系列（○五年）

《Box》装置展（○五年）

《香港春卷》漫画集展览（○五年）

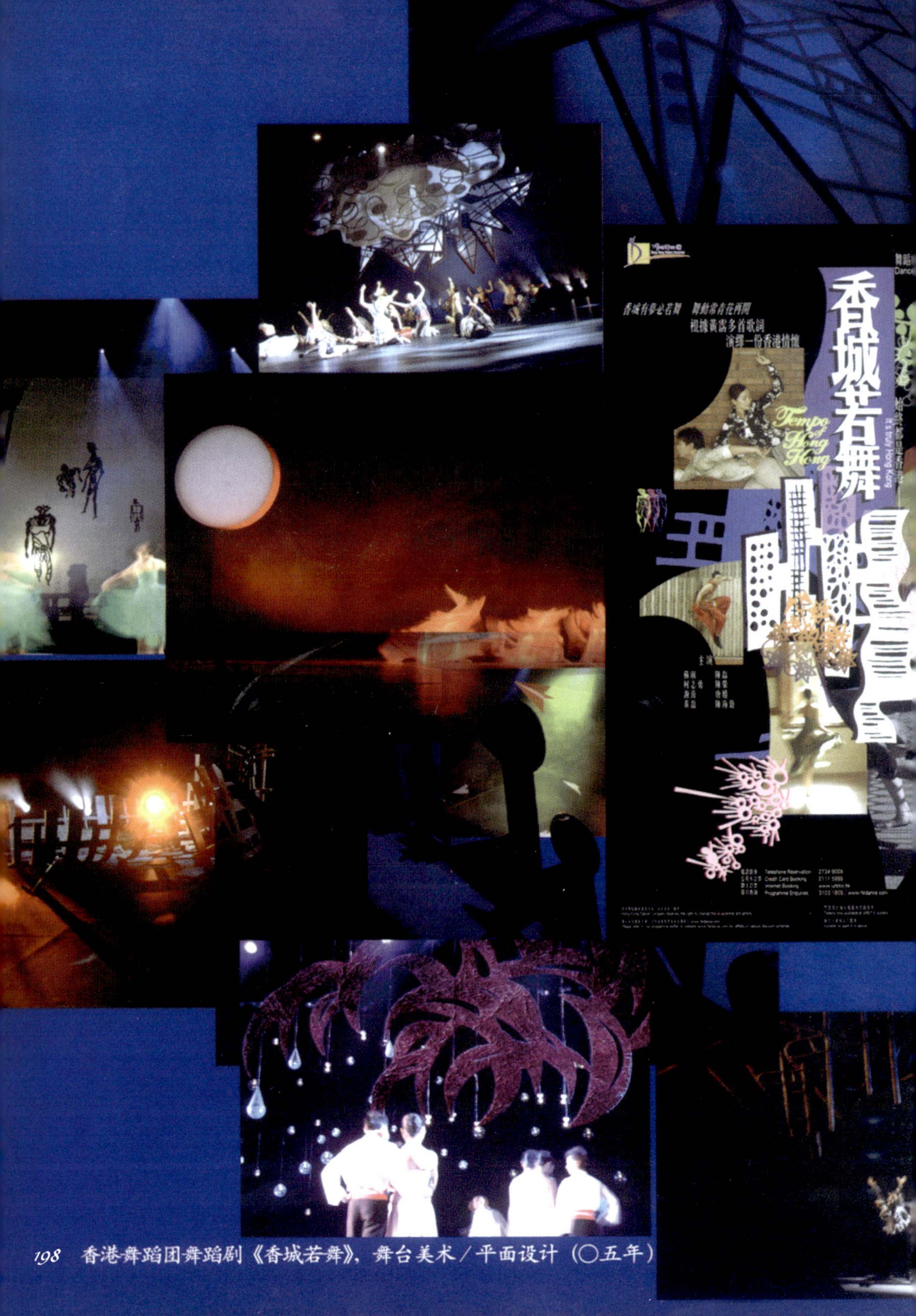

 香港舞蹈团舞蹈剧《香城若舞》，舞台美术／平面设计（〇五年）

欧阳应霁总是飞来飞去。
这个生活得飞来飞去的空中飞人，
原来有个人生最高指导原则：更有趣，要好玩！
绝大多数的时候，欧阳应霁无法评估所有他涉猎的工作孰重孰轻，
只知道在他专注于某件事时，那就是他当下的重心。
惟有到了年终，要跟自己算算总账之际，
才明白漫画毕竟是他创作领域里的锚，有着根深蒂固的基础，
其他的工作则是从这个核心逐渐向外蔓延。

—— 老嘉华 ○一年八月

后记

我愿意

记忆之中，竟然没有做过以《我的志愿》为题的文。

如果真的在小学三年级被迫着写这样的一个题目，
实在也不会是我手写我口，因为那个年纪根本就口不对心，
而我，分明从小就贪心，志愿肯定飘忽。

话说回来，我倒也从未立志做医生、警察、律师或者歌手、杀手，
也算是蛮早就很直接的把父母各自从事的画和写的专业加起来，
认定了自己写写画画的兴趣和能力，算是某种认命。

如今如果再来写一篇《我的志愿》，我会取巧的写《我的第一志愿》
——推开种种别的诱惑，我还是钟情写写画画，
而漫画，就是最完美最极致的图文结合。

喜欢漫画里图文呼应时的暧昧抽离，也过瘾于文图并茂的直接痛快。
作为一个读者，漫画同时是娱乐也是教化，

作为一个创作者，漫画就是能量的累积，然后爆发，欲仙欲死。

从报章密集投稿到自家连载专栏，
从《男儿汉》、《城市男人》、《故事新编》、《连环图》、
《我的天》、《三七廿一》到《小明》、《废画》、《我的天使》、
《爱到死》、《少年得志》……
二十多年来断断续续兜兜转转，
从绝无负担的很单纯的发表到自以为很周密的企划计算，
一意孤行但眼高手低未能挥洒自如，种种胡思乱想未能贯彻始终，
真是一种罪过也只能怪我。

如今小休过后再出发，有点百废待举的荒凉与兴奋——
在哪里跌倒（其实是困了睡着了），就在哪里站起来，
环顾四周暗呼我的天——
天变地变，那些拳打脚踢鼓励鞭策我的读者竟然还在——
为人为己，我在此起誓，我愿意，我会努力。

应霁　〇五年十月

图书在版编目(CIP)数据

我的我的天：应霁漫画前传/欧阳应霁著.－北京：生活·读书·新知三联书店，2006.1 （2006.6重印）（2012.2重印）
（home书系）
ISBN 978－7－108－02372－8

Ⅰ.我… Ⅱ.欧… Ⅲ.漫画：连环画－作品集－中国－当代 Ⅳ.I228.2

中国版本图书馆CIP数据核字(2005)第136639号

home书系　**我的我的天——应霁漫画前传**
欧阳应霁 著

责任编辑　郑　勇　詹那达
装帧设计　欧阳应霁　朱伟升
版面制作　崔建华　薛　宇
责任印制　卢　岳
出版发行　**生活·讀書·新知**三联书店
（北京市东城区美术馆东街22号）
邮　　编　100010
经　　销　新华书店
印　　刷　北京市松源印刷有限公司
版　　次　2006年1月北京第1版
2012年2月北京第3次印刷
开　　本　720毫米×965毫米　1/16　印张　12.875
字　　数　40千字　图　片　400幅
印　　数　13,001－18,000册
定　　价　28.00元